"Hello, Angela. So you're back."

Nate struggled to find a nonchalant tone. "That video you took out before you left is a tad overdue."

She planted one hand on a slender curving hip. "After ten years is that all you have to say to me?"

As if he should be the one to apologize. When they were married, half the time he hadn't known whether he wanted to strangle her or make love to her. Nothing had changed. She might have the face of an angel, but she had the devil's own ability to make him toss common sense to the winds. "I've got plenty to say, but not in a public place."

"Ah, the same old Nate." Angela started to turn away, then hesitated. "Ricky doesn't realize we were married. It might be easier if we kept it that way."

Now she was denying they were ever together. Was this it, then? Were they finally going to break the last flimsy tie between them?

Advantages of Bachelorhood Number 149: freedom.

Now that he thought about it, it sounded damn good.

Dear Reader,

Imagine a man so gutsy he launches his mountain bike down sheer rock face, so strong he cycles uphill for hours, so focused he wins every competition he enters. Then picture the woman who can turn his insides to mush with her smile, make his knees weak with her touch and forget his vow *never to fall for her again*.

Nate Wilde is that man and the woman is his runaway bride, Angela. *Homecoming Wife* is the first in a trilogy of stories set in Whistler, British Columbia, a rugged mountain resort famed for world-class outdoor sports.

Such a spectacular setting demands heroes who are larger than life, with uncommon physical and mental strength. Ride along with Nate as he faces the toughest challenge of his life—winning the love of his one special woman.

I love to hear from readers. Please write to me at P.O. Box 234, Point Roberts, WA 98281-0234, or send an e-mail via www.joankilby.com.

Sincerely,

Joan Kilby

Homecoming Wife
Joan Kilby

HARLEQUIN®

TORONTO • NEW YORK • LONDON
AMSTERDAM • PARIS • SYDNEY • HAMBURG
STOCKHOLM • ATHENS • TOKYO • MILAN • MADRID
PRAGUE • WARSAW • BUDAPEST • AUCKLAND

ISBN 0-373-71212-X

HOMECOMING WIFE

Copyright © 2004 by Joan Kilby.

This edition published by arrangement with Harlequin Books S.A.

® and TM are trademarks of the publisher. Trademarks indicated with ® are registered in the United States Patent and Trademark Office, the Canadian Trade Marks Office and in other countries.

www.eHarlequin.com

Printed in U.S.A.

To my beloved mother, Ruby Friesen. 1924–2003

I'm grateful to Kevan Kobyashi for information on
mountain biking in the Whistler area. Any errors are mine.
The biking trail in the book is part real, part fiction,
based on the needs of the story.

Several books on mountain biking proved invaluable in the
research for this book: *Mountain Biking British Columbia* (2nd
edition) by Steve Dunn, *Dirt!* by John Howard and *Mountain
Biking Skills* compiled by the editors of
Mountain Bike and *Bicycling* magazines.

Books by Joan Kilby

HARLEQUIN SUPERROMANCE
 777—A FATHER'S PLACE
 832—TEMPORARY WIFE
 873—SPENCER'S CHILD
 941—THE CATTLEMAN'S BRIDE
 965—THE SECOND PROMISE
1030—CHILD OF HIS HEART
1076—CHILD OF HER DREAMS
1114—CHILD OF THEIR VOWS

Don't miss any of our special offers. Write to us at the
following address for information on our newest releases.

Harlequin Reader Service
U.S.: 3010 Walden Ave., P.O. Box 1325, Buffalo, NY 14269
Canadian: P.O. Box 609, Fort Erie, Ont. L2A 5X3

CHAPTER ONE

ADVANTAGE OF BACHELORHOOD *Number 147: No
wife to disapprove of a man's passion for mountain
bikes.*

Nate Wilde added the latest item to his ongoing
mental list as he closed up his mountain-bike shop,
Cycle Sports, and strapped on his helmet. He'd
been compiling the list ever since the snowy
Whistler night a decade ago when Angela left him.
Technically speaking, he wasn't a bachelor because they were still married but for all practical
purposes he was on his own.

Nate got on his favorite bike, the Balfa Belair.
Blazing red with gold forks over the front wheel
and a sweet-looking seat tower arrangement, the
Balfa floated over the cobbled streets of Whistler
Village. Nate turned down a flight of concrete
stairs, causing a group of Japanese tourists to raise
their cameras and click madly.

His brother, Aidan, had he known about the list,
would have said Nate was rationalizing his loss.
His cousin, Marc, who'd grown up with them after
his mother died, would have told him he was full

of shit, but that's what happened when a guy married too young and too fast.

And Angela, the only woman he'd ever loved, would have put her nose in the air, sniffed and said "typical." If she'd stuck around long enough to say anything, that is. She'd believed neither in him nor their future together. He'd wanted kids; she'd been adamantly opposed. They'd been fighting over when to start a family the night she'd run off, breaking his heart and shattering his pride.

Barely a day went by when he didn't count his blessings that she was out of his life.

Barely a day went by when he didn't also wonder how she was, and what she was doing.

In fact, he knew what Angela was doing more or less all the time because her sister Janice had kept him up to date on the steady rise in Angela's fortunes since she left him. She'd studied business in Toronto then worked at the *Globe and Mail* newspaper until two months ago when she'd returned to Vancouver to take a high-powered job with a business magazine.

In all that time her only communication had been a brief phone call a month after her departure to say their marriage was a mistake followed by a garbled letter purporting to explain why she wasn't coming home but which left him no wiser.

His attempts to contact her through Janice had

failed, and he'd been forced to conclude she wanted nothing more to do with him.

How could she have left him simply because she wasn't ready to have a baby?

Cycling home on the highway, Nate remembered that his fridge was seriously depleted so he stopped in at Nester's Market to stock up on essentials.

Janice's latest news flash was that Angela was coming to Whistler to baby-sit her ten-year-old nephew, Ricky, while Janice and her husband, Bob, went on a short vacation. In a small community like Whistler there was no way Nate and Angela could avoid seeing each other so he'd been preparing himself in advance to keep a lid on his anger, a tight rein on his libido and a watchful eye out for any assault on his pride.

ANGELA HAULED ON the steering wheel of Janice's ancient green Dodge and the car lumbered around the tight curves on the Sea-to-Sky highway north of Vancouver. Mountains rose steeply to her right, the waters of Howe Sound lapped the shore to her left and signs warning of falling rocks appeared around every other bend. She'd seen her sister and brother-in-law off at the airport and now she and Ricky were heading back to Whistler.

Ricky had his head down and was stabbing away

at his Game Boy. His blond hair was gelled to spiky peaks and freckles smattered his straight nose. Below his shorts, both knees were scabbed over and Band-Aids, some clean, some grubby, plastered several fingers and an elbow.

If the baby she'd been carrying the night she ran away had lived, he or she would have been about the same age as Ricky.

Angela had pushed away similar thoughts for years; the closer she got to Whistler and Nate, the more frequently the baby came to mind. Would he have been athletic and full of pride like Nate, or ambitious and stubborn like her?

She didn't know much about kids in general, and she hadn't seen Ricky since he was an infant. Frankly, she was terrified of making mistakes with him. What if he didn't like her, or do what she told him to? What if he got hurt while under her care? According to Janice, he was both daring and accident-prone.

"What do you do for fun, Ricky?" she asked after her first few questions elicited only monosyllables.

"Ride my bike."

Three whole words. That was an improvement. When Janice and Bob had won a trip to Europe in a supermarket contest she'd gladly offered to babysit, not stopping to consider that taking care of a boy wasn't the same as watering a plant or even looking after a pet.

Cooking was another worry. If Ricky expected homemade meals every night he was in for an unpleasant surprise. "What do you like to eat?"

"Pizza." He glanced up from the miniature screen, leaving his fingers poised over the buttons. "Hamburgers."

"Great!" she said, relieved. "Those are my favorites, too."

"Ice cream," he went on loquaciously. "Candy, cookies, chips…that kind of stuff."

"We'll go shopping as soon as we get to Whistler."

Angela rolled down the window and breathed the fresh, pine-scented air. Ahead, she could see the towering peaks of Whistler and Blackcomb Mountains where even now in early July, glaciers glistened whitely in the brilliant blue sky. It felt good to be coming home.

But she was nervous, too, at the prospect of seeing Nate. How would he react to her after all this time?

Maybe if he hadn't loved his bikes more than he loved her they wouldn't have fought in the first place. Maybe if Nate had known she was pregnant he would have tried harder to stop her from leaving. Maybe if she hadn't run away she wouldn't have miscarried and they would be a family now instead of two people legally united but who barely knew each other.

That was a lot of maybes.

She'd been too young, too immature and too insecure to admit she was wrong and ask him to take her back. The bottom line was he'd let her go without a struggle.

Angela's hands felt stiff from being clenched around the steering wheel. She shook them until the blood returned to the knuckles and consciously tried to relax. She'd been in limbo for a decade, unable to settle. She'd always hoped that somehow she and Nate would get back together, but ten years had passed and neither had made the first move. So be it. Maybe their marriage *was* irrevocably damaged. Or maybe a spark existed of their former love.

One way or another, Angela thought, it was past time to resolve the situation.

LEAVING THE BALFA securely locked in front of Nester's, Nate moved through the produce section, bagging fresh vegetables and fruit and tossing them into his shopping cart. Yes, sir, bachelorhood had lots of advantages, including healthy food instead of the junk Angela favored.

He rounded the end of the aisle and suddenly his cart collided with another, startling him.

"Whoops, sorry." The grinning spiky-haired boy careening around the corner on the back of a loaded shopping cart looked anything but sorry.

"Careful, kid. You might have rammed an elderly lady instead of me. Hey, you're Ricky, aren't you?" Nate added, recognizing Janice's son. "Where's your mom? I thought she and your dad would be on their way to Europe by now."

"They are. Look, I can do a wheelie." Ricky, his feet planted on the frame, leaned back and pulled on the handle, causing the front of the cart to tip in the air.

"Ricky!" a woman called from the next aisle. "Where are you?"

Nate heard the voice and his heart jerked like a slipping bicycle gear.

An instant later Angela hurried around the aisle. "I'm so sorry about my nephew—" Seeing Nate she broke off as recognition dawned in her wide blue eyes. Polished fingertips raked through hair streaked with sunlight and honey. "Nate!"

"Hello, Angela. So you're back." He struggled to find a nonchalant tone. "That video you took out before you left is a tad overdue."

Her V-neck top and cropped pants looked casual but expensive; gold circled her wrist and neck and hung from her earlobes. Clearly Angela had attained for herself the financial security she hadn't believed him capable of.

Advantage of Bachelorhood Number 148: No extravagant wife to squander his hard-earned cash.

She planted one hand on a slender curving hip. "After ten years is that all you have to say to me?"

As if *he* should be the one to apologize. When they were married half the time he never knew whether he wanted to strangle her or make love to her. Nothing had changed. She might have the face of an angel but she had the devil's own ability to make him toss common sense to the winds. *Keep a lid on the anger,* he reminded himself.

"I've got plenty to say but not in a public place."

Her gaze dropped to the loose nylon shirt and reinforced shorts he wore for biking. "Are you still financing your hobby by working for your dad building log homes?"

Obviously, Janice didn't keep Angela as well informed about him. Despite Angela's lowly origins, or perhaps because of them, she'd been intensely dissatisfied with his apparent lack of ambition. Now that he was successful, he felt no inclination to justify himself to her. "I spend most of my time at the bike shop," he said ambiguously.

"Ah, the same old Nate." But she looked a little disappointed he'd lived *down* to her expectations.

"You look as though you've done well for yourself."

Her chin tilted upward at a confident angle. "I'm marketing director for *Businesswomen's Weekly,* a lifestyle magazine for professional women."

"Very impressive." He got the message. She was the same old Angela, too—tough as nails and in no need of him.

"It's a temporary position," she conceded. "The woman I'm replacing is on maternity leave but she may decide to stay away indefinitely in which case I'll be permanent."

The sound of tin cans falling over made Angela hurry on ahead. Ricky, one foot on the lower shelf, one hand gripping the top shelf, looked their way guiltily as canned tomatoes rolled at his feet.

"Ricky! Are you hurt?" Angela exclaimed as she reached his side. "If you want something from a higher shelf you should ask someone. What are you after?"

"Nothin'." He hopped off the shelf and ran off down the aisle, leaving Angela frowning after him in frustration.

Nate came over, pushing both carts. "You'd better put the brakes on that boy before he takes complete control.''

''I'm perfectly capable of looking after my own nephew, thank you. Ricky's just...high-spirited.''

Nate glanced at the assortment of cookies and doughnuts in her cart. ''Sugar will do that to a kid.''

She took the cart from him and wheeled away. ''I don't need your advice.''

Nate followed. ''I understand you're looking after Ricky while Janice and Bob are in Europe. What prompted this outburst of familial devotion?''

''Janice and Bob haven't had a vacation in years.''

''What about your job?''

''With e-mail and occasional trips to Vancouver I can work from here for a month.''

''A month!'' Nate stopped in his tracks. ''I thought their prize was a trip to seven countries in as many days.''

''A week seemed too rushed so they extended their vacation.''

''A month in Europe. Sweet. And expensive.'' Janice was a waitress and Bob drove the shuttle bus that ferried skiers and sightseers between chairlifts. Nate had gotten the impression they were just scraping by.

"I helped them a little," Angela said offhandedly. They came to the frozen-foods section and she paused to load some pizzas into the cart.

"You really haven't changed," Nate observed with a pointed glance at the pizza.

"There's something different about you, though...." Wearing a puzzled frown, Angela paused and studied his face. Then she reached up to stroke one of his sideburns with her cool fingertips. "These are new."

"What do you think?" He no sooner spoke than he wanted to kick himself for implying her opinion still mattered to him.

She took his jaw between her fingers and turned his face from side to side. Her perfume tickled his nostrils with memories and her touch was a torment. *Play it cool, Wilde. And for God's sake, keep that libido under control.*

"I like them," she said at last. "They're kind of sexy."

Sexy.

"How've you been?" he asked, and at that moment his voice decided to go all husky on him. He hoped he wouldn't make an idiot of himself but with Angela there was no guarantee things would proceed according to plan.

Her gaze connected with his. "I've been okay. You?"

She dumped you, remember? Hardening his tone, he replied, "Great. Just great."

Abruptly, her hand dropped from his jaw, as if she'd just realized what she was doing. "We need to talk. About us. Get things sorted out."

"I agree." He pushed his cart forward, remembering at the last minute to pick up some frozen juice. Angela could make him forget his own name if she looked at him the right way.

"You never wanted to marry again?" she asked conversationally as they moved into the next aisle.

He shook his head. "Some might say you scarred me for life."

"Or spoiled you for anyone else." She glanced sideways as if to see how he'd react to this and there was actually a twinkle in her eye.

Well, he wasn't going to bite. He grunted and reached for a jar of pasta sauce to place in his cart.

"What about girlfriends?" Her words were delivered coolly, as if in only passing interest.

"Presently, no." Something about her carefully averted profile made him ask, "Why? Do you want me back? Is that why you came to Whistler?"

"Oh! You are *so* arrogant." She pushed her cart purposefully down the aisle. "I wonder where Ricky is."

Nate thought about heading in the opposite direction but he refused to go out of his way to avoid further contact. It would look as though he couldn't handle being with her. Following at a slower pace he caught up with Angela and Ricky in the confectionery aisle. Ricky was pulling bags of candy off the shelves and dumping them into Angela's shopping cart.

"Not too many, Ricky," Angela was saying. "Candy causes tooth decay."

Unfazed by her remonstrations, Ricky tossed another bag into the cart.

"Sugar can also lead to diabetes and obesity," Angela continued to reason unsuccessfully with the boy. "It stops you from eating more nutritious food."

"Like pizza?" Nate couldn't help interject.

Angela glared at him.

Ricky shrugged and pulled away from her. "I don't care. It tastes good."

Nate grasped the boy gently but firmly by the shoulder and turned Ricky around to face him. "While your aunt is looking after you, you do what she says. Now put all but one bag of candy back on the shelves."

"You're not in charge of me," Ricky argued.

"*Put it back.*" Nate gazed steadily into the boy's eyes. "Understand?"

"Yessir," Ricky mumbled and squirmed out of

Nate's grip. Reluctantly he began to return the candy to the shelf.

Angela grabbed Nate by the arm and dragged him a few feet away. "How dare you interfere?" she demanded in a furious undertone. "I told you I would handle my nephew."

Nate snorted. "Kids have to be taught limits. I'll bet Janice doesn't let him get away with stuff."

"I suppose *you're* an expert on children?"

"I have a young niece, and I work with kids, many of them from troubled homes."

"Since when?"

"Since after you left. You know, an organized activity would help keep Ricky out of trouble." Nate turned to Ricky who was kicking the wheels of the cart, bored with waiting for the adults. "Hey, dude. Do you like mountain bikes? I teach a course for ten to twelve-year-olds."

"Mountain biking!" Ricky stopped kicking the wheels and perked up. "That would be so cool. I think my friend, Tim, is taking your course."

"Tim Martin? Yes, he is." Nate used to date Tim's mother, Kerry, although for some months now they'd just been friends. "The course begins next week with classes on Tuesday and Friday. Do you have a mountain bike?" Ricky nodded. "Bring it down to Cycle Sports in the Village and my mechanic will check it over for you."

"Wait just a minute!" Angela protested. "If you think I'm handing this unsuspecting child over to you, the king of daredevils himself, you're nuts."

"With appropriate precautions and proper training, mountain biking is perfectly safe," Nate said, irritated.

"Oh, yeah? Remember the time you hit a boulder coming down Blackcomb Mountain and snapped your collarbone? Or the time you broke your arm when your bike hit a big root?"

Ricky listened eagerly, eyes round, mouth parted.

"I was riding tech trails, training for competitions." Nate explained what Angela should have known perfectly well. "If Ricky doesn't have protective gear I've got extra pads he can borrow."

"And what about that close encounter with a spruce tree which ended with fifteen stitches?" She stood on tiptoe to peer at his right cheekbone. "I can still see the scar."

"I don't do stunts anymore and I haven't had a serious injury in years." He paused. "I stopped racing."

That took her aback. "You gave up racing?"

Her skepticism wasn't unfounded; for years racing had consumed him. He shrugged. "My priorities changed."

"Too little, too late," she muttered. "Come on,

Ricky.'' She walked away again, dragging Ricky by the hand while the boy looked longingly over his shoulder at Nate.

Fine, let her go. This time he wouldn't follow. Nate lifted a hand in farewell. ''Catch you later, dude.''

Nate finished his shopping and went through the checkout. By the time he'd packed his groceries into his empty backpack and unchained the Balfa, Angela was coming out of the store. Realizing that if they were going to talk they had to arrange a time and place, he followed her to her car.

While Ricky goggled at the Balfa, Angela opened the trunk of her car and began to lift bags inside. Her gaze flicked to the clouds massing above the mountains. ''It looks like rain.''

Nate helped her load groceries and cast an educated eye over the sky. ''The cumulus are building but higher up in the stratosphere winds are brisk. I don't think we'll see any rain until later tonight.''

Ricky took his awestruck gaze off the bike to peer up at Nate. ''You sound like the weatherman on TV.''

''I study meteorology in my spare time.'' Nate caught Angela's surprised glance and added, ''When you're on a bike, facing a sheer drop off a mountain ridge, you want to know which way the wind blows.''

"Cool,'' Ricky breathed. "Aunt Angela, I *gotta* go mountain biking.''

"Meteorology?'' Angela repeated, ignoring her nephew. "Does this mean you finally decided on a direction in life?''

"It's a hobby. Doesn't Janice tell you anything?''

"She didn't mention *that*.'' She pushed her cart into the trolley bay and moved toward the driver's side of the Dodge.

"You wanted to talk,'' Nate said. He'd waited a long time for the chance to thrash things through; the sooner they got it over, the better. He glanced at Ricky who was watching them with avid curiosity. How much did the boy know about their situation?

Angela casually turned to her nephew. "Hop in the car, Ricky.''

Ricky glanced at Nate, Nate nodded imperceptibly, and the boy got in the passenger seat. Angela frowned at Ricky's deference to Nate then seemed to shake off her irritation with an effort. "Where do we start?''

"How about with you running away?'' He spoke forcefully, forgetting all good intentions about keeping his anger under control. "What the hell was that about?"

"We had a fight if you recall. You were pressuring me to start a family but you and your bike always came first. Face it, we weren't even ready to marry. I was nineteen and you were twenty—way too young."

"We had very different ideas of what marriage entailed, that's for sure. I was in it for the long haul whereas you gave up when the going got rough."

"It wasn't like that," she said indignantly.

"You can't argue with the facts. You only lasted a few months. Then when we fought you didn't stick around to talk things out. Instead, you left me."

"You let me go." For an instant her features contorted in pain. Her eyes closed briefly and when she opened them again her face was composed. "Obviously you didn't care enough to try to find me."

"I *did* try, the next day, after I realized you'd gone to Vancouver and not to Janice's. I couldn't find you in any of the places she suggested looking. Where were you?"

She looked away, one hand gripping the car roof. "Okay, I admit that at first I told Janice not to tell you where I was—"

He threw his hands up. "And you blame me for our breakup."

"—then I changed my mind, but you'd gone back to your stupid bike race."

"Because it never occurred to me you would leave me for good. The prize money was a considerable chunk of dough—well, it seemed like it at the time—and I figured we would need it if we were going to start a family."

Angela paled under her tan as she stared at him in silence. A moment later she was back on the attack. "How could we have afforded a baby with you spending all your money and time with your bikes?"

"That was an investment that paid off."

"How was I to know that? I didn't want any kid of mine growing up the way I did, nor did I want to end up a single mom in a trailer park if you got yourself killed falling off the mountain." She wagged a finger at him. "Don't tell me it doesn't happen because I know it does."

"You never had any faith in me. If we'd had a baby do you really believe I would have let you and the child want for anything?"

"I don't know and that's the whole point. You were always off on your bike. The day after I left, instead of coming looking for me you were riding in some competition! I know bikes are important to you but they shouldn't have been more important than *me!*"

"They weren't! And if you hadn't stayed away we might have worked out our differences." That remark was met with a strained silence. Nate shook his head. They were going around in circles. "Now that you're back, where do we go from here?"

Drawing a deep breath, she said, "We've been separated for ten years. It's time to resolve the past and move on with our lives."

His insides seemed to freeze. "Are you talking about a divorce?"

Her fingers twisted the strap on her purse. Her eyes were very bright. "Is that what you want?"

"Does it matter what I want?" he asked bitterly. After all this time the suggestion to make their split permanent and legal shouldn't come as a surprise but somehow he wasn't prepared for it. "Are you planning to marry again? Janice told me you were seeing someone in Toronto." Damn. He sounded like a jealous husband.

"This has nothing to do with Albert. That's over."

A retired couple pulled their cart up at the camper van parked next to Angela and started loading groceries. Frustrated, Nate said, "We'd better finish this later. I'll call you tonight."

Angela started to turn away, then hesitated.

"Ricky doesn't realize we were married. It might be easier if we kept it that way."

Now she was denying they were ever together. She got in her car and drove away, leaving Nate feeling as if he'd just cycled straight into a rock wall at eighty miles an hour.

He slung on his backpack, strapped on his helmet and pedaled off. Flipping the Shimano gears into a higher sprocket, he coasted down the ramp onto the highway with the wind in his ears.

Was this it, then? Were they finally going to break the last flimsy tie between them?

Advantage of Bachelorhood Number 149: Freedom.

Now that he thought about it, it sounded damn good.

CHAPTER TWO

"WHAT WOULD YOU RATHER EAT, a caterpillar or a moth?" Ricky said as if this was the most reasonable question in the world.

Angela was tidying the kitchen after dinner, or rather, attempting to, since her mind was flitting between her earlier encounter with Nate and their coming conversation. The wall calendar bearing the legend Wilde Log Home Construction that kept catching her eye didn't help. Now she stared at Ricky, not certain she'd heard correctly. "I don't know. What would *you* rather eat?"

"A caterpillar, of course," Ricky replied. "It's juicy and a moth is yucky and dry, like feathers."

"I see." She was not going to ask him how he knew.

Getting out the broom, she swept up the crumbs of their pizza from beneath the table. Janice's house, with its pine furniture and cheaply framed photos, wasn't anything fancy, but rag rugs, polished floorboards and chunky handmade pottery gave it a warm, comfortable feel. However, the clutter also made it difficult to clean and Angela spared a wistful thought for her immaculate minimalist apartment in Vancouver.

When she was done sweeping Angela set up her laptop on the kitchen table so she could work on her marketing plan for the next quarter while she waited for Nate to call.

Ricky moved closer and eyed her computer with interest. "Do you have any games on there?" She shook her head. "Tim's got a computer with a ton of games," he went on. "Dad said we'll get a computer for Christmas. If we can afford it."

"Uh-huh," Angela said absently as she organized her notes while the laptop booted up. Then she realized Ricky was still watching her. "I guess my work can wait until tomorrow. Would you like to play a board game?"

"Board games are boring," Ricky said. "I'd rather play with my Game Boy."

"I don't have one so we couldn't play together."

"How about cars?" he suggested.

"Grown women don't play with cars unless they're full-size luxury models," she said, attempting a joke. Ricky didn't crack a smile and she wondered fleetingly if kids, like dogs, could tell when a person was nervous around them.

"I'll just go watch TV." With a resigned sigh

he went down the hall to the living room leaving Angela feeling as though she'd failed him some-how.

With a sigh of her own she inserted a disk into her computer and called up the file containing the spreadsheet of this month's advertising expenditures. Again her fingers hovered over the keyboard, ready to type, but her thoughts had returned to Nate.

All the way to Whistler she'd tried to steel herself for their first meeting but she hadn't been prepared for the leap of her heart when she'd rounded the aisle and seen him standing there, a bag of muesli in his hand. His thick dark hair was still perennially tousled, as though he'd just taken his bike helmet off and run his hands through it. And he was as combative as when they'd been together. Back then they'd engaged in battles of wits as naturally as breathing, as frequently as lovemaking.

She could still recall the day they'd met. She'd been taking her break out back of the Whistler hotel where she worked as a chambermaid when he'd wheeled down the lane after winning a bike race, buzzing with testosterone and adrenaline.

With his hair falling over his forehead, tanned forearms and powerful thighs, she recognized him as one of the Wilde boys. Wilde by name, wild by nature. He was from a comfortably well-off family, not the type to notice a poor girl from Pemberton, a logging town half an hour north of the resort. Yet he'd stopped, made her laugh with his teasing banter, then asked her what time she got off.

"Why?" She'd wanted to know.

"I'd like to get to know you." He stopped circling the lane, planted his feet on the ground and looked straight at her. "Angela."

It was the way he spoke her name that got her— courteous, appreciative, attentive.

He'd laughed at her smart-assed comments and dished his own right back, yet he gave her the respect she'd always craved and hadn't pressed when she refused to sleep with him before marriage even though they were going crazy for each other. Folks might think she came from trash but, by God, no one would ever have cause to say she had loose morals.

Funny thing, though, smart as Nate was, he'd never figured out that her tough act was all a facade.

Would he ask for a divorce or propose reconciliation? For her to suggest they get back together wasn't an option; she simply wasn't brave enough to risk rejection. Nate had loved her because he thought she was strong and fearless. Even now, when it might be over—especially now—she couldn't, wouldn't, let him see how vulnerable she was.

It was an uncomfortable thought and enough to send her back to the spreadsheet on the computer screen. Busy with figures and plans, the evening slipped away.

NATE HANDED A BEER to his brother, Aidan, twisted the top off his own, then tilted back in his chair and plunked his boots on the top rail of his balcony. He'd built the log house himself in Alpine Meadows estate off Alta Lake Road, three years after Angela left.

Advantage of Bachelorhood Number 150: Resting booted feet wherever the hell he liked. It wasn't one of his best, but hey, some days he took what he could get.

"I ran into Angela today," he told Aidan. "She's in town looking after her nephew."

Aidan cast him a shrewd sideways glance. His wavy brown hair tapered to the collar of a shirt the same green as his eyes. "That must have been a shock. How long has it been—ten years?"

Nate nodded. "It was a surprise, all right. She wants a divorce."

Eyebrows raised, Aidan gave a low whistle. "I've always wondered why you haven't gotten one before this."

"I never found anyone else I wanted to marry,"
Nate said with a shrug. "I presumed the same was
true for her, even though she was going with some
guy in Toronto."

"So does this mean now she wants to remarry?"

"She *says* not." Nate reached for a handful of
dried fruit and nuts from the bowl on the table
between them. "She says it's time for us to get on
with our lives."

"Maybe she's right," Aidan mused. "You've
always wanted a family and you're not going to
get one while married to a woman you don't live
with."

"Yeah, I guess." He stared out over the valley.
Below, a shaft of the setting sun broke through the
dark clouds to reflect off a bend in the poetically
named River of Golden Dreams, a slow-moving
stream that meandered through low bushes between Alta Lake and Green Lake, flanked by the
paved Valley Trail.

Aidan sipped his beer. "What did she say? How
did she seem?"

Nate summarized the encounter for him, finishing, "She was just so...*Angela.*"

Aidan smiled. "Sassy? Sexy?"

Nate breathed out on a long sigh. Angela was to
sexy what scent was to a rose, what juice was to
a mango. She was also strong, ambitious and de-

termined. A late riser, a junk-food eater, a smart-mouthed runaway bride. Okay, newlywed; counting their whirlwind courtship they'd lasted nearly six months.

"You're still in love with her," Aidan said, making his own deductions from Nate's silence.

Jolted out of his thoughts, Nate twisted around in his chair to glare at Aidan. He'd never told anyone he pined for Angela, not even his family. He had his pride. "Why would you say a thing like that?"

Aidan chuckled. "You poor deluded sap. You should hear yourself when you talk about her."

His brother's jibe irritated Nate. "When you get over Charmaine long enough to pull down all the froufrou and lace in your house then you can talk to me about Angela."

Aidan's smile faded. His focus dropped to the bottle he twisted between clenched hands. "Charmaine—" He broke off, unable to speak of his late wife, dead these past six years.

Nate winced at his thoughtless cruelty. "Sorry, buddy, that was out of line. As for Angela, no way am I still in love with her. Nor will I make the mistake of falling in love with her again."

Aidan gave him a disbelieving glance and wisely skirted away from the subject of wives. "Have you heard from Marc lately?"

"Mom got a letter from him yesterday. Apparently he's in Pakistan trying to round up a cameraman brave enough to venture into the tribal areas with him. I've heard the police won't even go in there." Nate shook his head in dismay. They sometimes joked that Marc had a death wish because he sought out the most dangerous spots on the planet to go looking for a story. Nate met Aidan's gaze. The joke just wasn't funny anymore, if it ever had been. "One of these days his luck's going to run out."

Aidan took a swig of beer. "He's going to try to make it back for Mom's birthday this weekend."

"That would be good." Nate paused, then asked after Aidan's young daughter. "How's Emily?"

"She can ride her two-wheeler without trainers, and she's already getting excited about starting first grade in the fall." Aidan dug through the remaining nuts to pick out the cashews. "What *are* you going to do about Angela? Will you contest the divorce?"

"I doubt if I have any grounds to do so." Nate blew softly into the top of his beer bottle, sending out a haunting sound that mingled with the sweet tinkle of the wind chimes at the end of the balcony. Dusk had come early and with it, the rain. A few drops fell onto the rail, making dark round splotches on the wood.

Setting the bottle aside, he said, "Angela dumped me in the most hurtful way possible, not to mention she makes me crazy. But here's the thing…when I'm with her, I feel alive in a way I never do without her. She brings more excitement to my day than the adrenaline rush of the slickest single track."

Aidan frowned, trying to understand. "I thought you said you weren't in love with her. Are you telling me you *are* going to attempt to reconcile?"

Before Nate could reply, the squall broke in a noisy rush and spattered the balcony with soaking rain. Nate and Aidan quickly gathered up their bottles and dragged the chairs under the overhanging roof. Nate glanced at his watch. After nine o'clock. It wasn't too late to call Angela but he felt drained and too confused to tangle with her on the phone. Tomorrow would do.

He brushed the water off his head and noticed Aidan was watching him, still waiting for an answer.

"If I make a mistake once, I can learn from it," Nate said. "Make the same mistake twice and I'd be a fool, wouldn't I?"

"Yeah, I guess," Aidan said. "Too bad, though. I always thought you two were great together."

So had Nate. He sighed. "Some things just aren't meant to be."

ANGELA LEANED BACK from her laptop, yawning and stretching. Ricky was being awfully quiet. Then she glanced at the clock. Could it really be eleven p.m.?

Nate hadn't called.

She saved her work and, pushing back her chair, went to the living room. Ricky was asleep on the couch in front of the TV where a movie unsuitable for ten-year-olds was playing. Recriminations flooded through her. She shouldn't have let him stay up this late. She should have monitored what he was watching.

"Ricky, wake up. It's time to go to bed."

The boy yawned and mumbled sleepily. "Just a little longer."

"No, it's after eleven." Angela reached for the control and clicked the TV off. In the silence she could hear the patter of raindrops being blown against the windowpane. "Tomorrow we'll do something fun, I promise."

Suddenly he looked wide awake, a crafty light in his eyes. "Mom always reads to me before bed."

"But it's so late."

"I'm on holiday."

"Aren't you old enough to read by yourself?" She suspected he was stalling but she couldn't be sure. Janice had left pages of detailed instructions regarding Ricky that Angela hadn't had time to go over yet.

"Yeah, but I like it when Mom reads."

"Oh, what the heck. Go get ready for bed first."

Ricky disappeared down the hall and came back a few minutes later dressed in his pajamas and smelling of toothpaste and soap. He looked sweet, not terrifying at all.

Angela followed him to his bedroom and sat on the bed. "Do you have a book?" she asked, expecting him to produce something like *Lassie Come Home*.

He handed her a slim volume with a lurid cover. She read the title. "*The Day My Bum Went Psycho?* Are you serious?"

"It's really funny."

"I'll read one chapter, okay?"

She ended up reading five chapters because Ricky kept pleading for more and because the zany story was surprisingly amusing. Finally her throat got sore and she set the book aside. "Time to say your prayers." That much she knew Janice insisted on.

Ricky hopped out from under the covers and kneeled by the bed, bowing his head. "Now I lay me down to sleep…'' His high-pitched voice mingled with the steady beat of rain on the shake roof.

Angela listened, remembering herself and Janice at a very young age as they kneeled by their cots on a threadbare rug to repeat those familiar comforting words.

''…God bless Mom and Dad and keep them safe on the airplane. God bless Auntie Angela and keep *me* safe so she doesn't worry.''

Angela smiled but she had to glance away; Ricky's slender nape above his pajama collar looked so vulnerable it made her heart hurt. When had she stopped saying her prayers? Probably around her seventh birthday when her father walked out and her mom started drinking and Angela had learned prayers didn't get answered. Night after night she'd comforted her little sister, pretending to Janice that everything would be all right when inside she felt terrified and utterly abandoned.

Why hadn't Nate called?

''…God bless Tim and keep him safe so…well, just so he'll be safe. Thank you, Lord. Amen.''

Ricky clambered back into bed and Angela wondered if he would hate it if she tried to kiss him good-night. She tickled him instead, making him giggle.

On impulse she said, "Tomorrow we'll go down and register you for the bike course."

She thought he would be delighted but his young forehead furrowed with worry. "How are we going to pay for it?" he asked. "I heard Dad tell Mom before they left that they were so far over dawn they'd never see daylight again. It doesn't make sense but I'm pretty sure he was talking about money 'cuz he had his checkbook out."

"He meant *overdrawn*." She bit her lip to stop herself from smiling at his mistake. There was nothing funny about a kid having to worry about his family's finances.

How often in her own childhood had her mother told her they couldn't afford something? Daily, at least. Not things like mountain-bike courses or the latest fashion, but more basic items like exercise books for school or shoes. Sometimes they couldn't even afford food until the next welfare check. Even though her mother was long dead and those days far behind her, Angela could still remember the shame.

"Don't worry. I'll pay for the course as an early birthday present. And I'll buy you your own elbow and shin pads so you can use them afterward."

Ricky's face lit. He sat up in bed and flung his arms around her waist, pressing his head against her chest. "Thank you, Auntie Angela. Thank you so much!"

Angela, treasuring the feel of his small body, clung a moment too long and he squirmed out of her embrace. "Quit calling me 'Auntie,'" she scolded to cover her awkwardness. "It makes me feel a hundred years old instead of twenty-nine. Just Angela will do."

"Okay. Thanks, Angela. You're the best."

"You're welcome." At least she'd gotten *something* right where he was concerned.

The next morning Angela and Ricky drove into Whistler Village with Ricky's bike in the back of the station wagon. They parked in one of the day lots and walked the bike through the pedestrian-only streets, looking for Nate's store.

Cycle Sports was a long narrow shop off the Village Square. Bikes were hung around the perimeter, shock absorbers and wheel forks covered the ceiling and every inch of available floor space was packed with rows of tires or shelving containing biking shirts, shorts, gloves and other paraphernalia. Customers browsed or stood about in small groups, talking trails and bikes. Nate wasn't the only one around here obsessed with mountain biking.

Ricky gravitated to a shiny new bike set up on display. Angela went to the front desk where a girl with short blond braids was stocking a display of sunglasses. Dressed in a halter top and lycra shorts she had the slim, hard body of an athlete and a killer tan.

"Excuse me...Rachel," Angela said, glancing at the girl's name tag. "I'm looking for Nate. Is he working today?"

"I'll get him for you." Rachel poked her head through a curtained doorway behind the desk. "Hey, boss. Someone to see you."

Boss. A blunt-fingered hand pushed the curtain aside and Nate appeared, his dark hair a sharp contrast to the pale blue of his bike shirt. Even after all this time he still set her pulse racing.

"Are you the manager here?" she asked incredulously.

"I own the store." There was more than a hint of satisfaction in his voice.

Angela vaguely recalled Janice saying something about a bike store but when it came to Nate and mountain bikes she'd always tuned out. She couldn't get over the change in him from the free and easy young man she'd married. Back then he'd worked only until he had enough to pay the bills, sometimes not even that much in the prelude to a big race. Now she marveled at Nate's confident air of authority—a maturation of his youthful cockiness she hadn't anticipated.

"Can I help you with something?" he asked.

"I've been thinking your class might be good for Ricky, after all. We've brought in his bike for you to look over."

Ricky, hearing his name, came over to where they were standing. Nate handed him a brochure of the Whistler Bike Park. "Check that out, dude." Then he signaled to a young man with burnished gold dreadlocks. "Chris, could you get down a ladies' bike for Angela, here, to try out?" His gaze traveled expertly over her five-foot-five frame. "Twenty-two inch, hardtail."

"Angela, listen to this," Ricky exclaimed, showing her the brochure. "The bike park has over four thousand vertical feet of trails."

Angela shuddered at this frightening mental image. "More than I need to know, thanks." As Chris moved to the rack of hanging bikes, she protested to Nate, "We're here for Ricky, not me."

Nate smiled at Angela. "Don't worry. We'll take care of you both." Turning to the boy, he went on, "Ricky, why don't you take your bike through to the workshop. Kevin, my mechanic, will look after you."

"Okay." Ricky shoved the brochure into his pocket and headed back outside where he'd left his bike chained to a stand.

Chris wheeled a silver-and-blue bike to where Angela and Nate were standing.

"Thanks, Chris," Nate said to his employee. "Kevin is going to check over Ricky's bike. Make sure the boy finds his way to the workshop, will you?"

"No problem." Chris moved off.

Angela glanced about; the store was abuzz with bike talk and the steady ka-ching of the credit-card machine. She didn't know much about mountain bikes but from the price tags she could tell these were top of the line. "Your store seems prosperous. I'm impressed." She paused. "And, I must confess, a little surprised."

Nate flipped a lever on the bike and lowered the seat. "I'm opening another store soon in Vancouver." He gave her a wry smile. "Turns out I'm a lot better at business than I ever was at carpentry. Ironic, eh?"

Angela glanced away from the dry expression in his eyes, and the implied reproach for not believing in him.

Nate put a hand on her arm and guided her to the bike. "Put a leg across so I can check the stand-over height."

Angela, still surprised by this new Nate, complied before she realized what she was doing. But when he crouched to inspect the gap between her and the silver steel tubing she hopped off. "I thought you were going to call me last night."

He shot her a quick glance. "Sorry about that. Aidan came over and we had a few beers. I…lost track of time."

He'd forgotten about her. Again, but so what? She'd been gone so long she couldn't expect to be top of Nate's list. Just as he wasn't on top of hers. "How *is* your brother?"

"He's…okay." Nate added in an undertone, "Do you know about Charmaine?"

"Janice told me she lost her bearings on top of Whistler Mountain during a blizzard and fell to her death. I'm so sorry."

"Aidan was with her." Nate paused as if uncomfortable with what he had to say but compelled to go on. "People talked. There was a lot of rumor and speculation…."

She knew what he was trying to tell her and her heart went out to him, Aidan and their whole family. "Aidan *adored* Charmaine. He would have done everything in his power to save her." Angela spoke with total conviction, squeezing his arm to emphasize her support.

Nate nodded, looking both relieved and grateful she'd taken that point of view. For a split second they were almost like a couple again. Then he set the bike to one side and said, "Let's go find Ricky."

Angela followed him across the store and around a partition to the workshop. Ricky was standing beside his upside-down bicycle watching Kevin, ultracool in silver-framed dark glasses and a choker made of links from a bike chain, adjust the brakes.

"I also teach the class basic repair and maintenance," Nate told her. "Ricky will learn to do more than just careen down a hill."

Angela nodded. Nate had always been fanatical about maintaining his bikes. "What about safety?"

"Mountain biking is about enjoying the outdoors and gaining confidence in your physical and mental abilities, not about breaking your neck doing kamikaze stunts."

"Couldn't have proved that by you when we first met," she said dryly.

"I was young and foolish. Everybody grows up sooner or later." His gaze raked over her. "Don't they?"

She lifted her chin. "The smart ones do."

"You learn to take calculated risks," he went on. "With solid technique training and experience the kids in my classes push themselves beyond what they ever thought possible. If they're really good they'll get hooked on the whole mind-body fusion.''

''Zen and the art of mountain biking?'' she said, eyebrows raised.

''More like Jedi-master training.'' His dark eyes twinkled but she knew he wasn't entirely joking. When he was cycling hard, deep in the zone, she knew he went to someplace she couldn't follow, could hardly fathom.

Then his expression sobered and he jerked his head, motioning for her to follow as he moved a few paces away. Angela cast a glance back at Ricky as she did so, but he was fully absorbed in watching Kevin.

In a low voice Nate asked, ''So what's involved in a divorce?''

They were back to that. How quickly he'd leaped at the idea of making their split up permanent and legal. ''I...I looked into the procedure. I've got all the documents ready. If I file—''

''*If?*''

She searched his eyes. *Help me out here, Nate. Give me a reason not to do this.* Seconds ticked by in silence. Nothing. ''*When,*'' she amended heavily. ''You then have a couple of weeks in which to contest it. I've got to warn you, my lawyer told me you don't have any grounds.''

''Don't worry.'' He crossed his arms over his

chest. "Life's too short to try to win the same woman over and over again."

"What is that supposed to mean?" she demanded.

"You figure it out."

Dismissing his cryptic comments, she went on. "Once the appeal period is finished I file the actual petition for divorce and we wait for the judge to make a decision. That's little more than a formality—we wouldn't even have to go to court."

"How very convenient." For some inexplicable reason, that seemed to make him angry. "Easy come, easy go."

"It is, isn't it?" she said coldly. "A matter of weeks and it will all be over." She paused and studied his set expression. "This doesn't mean we have to end up enemies. Unless you *enjoy* battling me."

Suddenly he gave a snort of genuine amusement. "Maybe I do. It's been a long time since I've had a sparring partner of your caliber. You're almost as much fun as an ex as you were when we were married."

"I'm not sure that's a compliment." But she couldn't suppress a reluctant smile. Good Lord. Their relationship hadn't changed—it still had as many ups and downs as one of Nate's precious bike trails, rolling swiftly from confrontation to humor and back again. No wonder it had taken her ten years to recover from the first time around—if this state of semiconstant agitation she felt when around him could be called recovery.

She glanced again at her nephew and changed the subject. "I'm not totally convinced this bike course is a good idea. If something happens to Ricky while he's in my care I'll never forgive myself. Janice will never forgive me. I'm going to worry the entire time he's on the mountain."

"Why do you think I got that bike out for you?" he said. "I know you're concerned about Ricky's safety. You can tag along with the class and make sure he's okay."

Angela uttered a short incredulous laugh. "Me, go mountain biking? You're crazy."

Nate shrugged. "If you don't have the guts..."

Darn him. He knew she never backed away from a challenge. Well, two could play at that game. *He* hated having his integrity questioned. "Why would I need guts when you told me it's not dangerous. Were you lying?"

"Maybe you're afraid of more than physical danger," he growled. "Maybe you're afraid of spending time around me in case you find that what you really want is to have me back."

Part of her had been hoping he would tease and cajole her into admitting she didn't want to make their separation permanent. But this wasn't good enough; he wasn't giving away any of his own feelings. "You wish!"

Nate strode over to a filing cabinet against the far wall, whipped out an application form and placed it in front of her. His expression was a mixture of challenge and triumph. "Sign up, then."

"Oh! You haven't changed," she said with an exasperated laugh. "You're still the same arrogant bastard you always were. But I'll do this to spend time with my nephew." She scribbled her signature at the bottom of the sheet of paper and threw the form back at him, maddened and at the same time highly stimulated by the exchange. "There. Satisfied?"

One corner of Nate's full mouth curled up. "For now."

CHAPTER THREE

"CAN I RIDE OVER TO TIM'S HOUSE?" Ricky asked after lunch. "I want to tell him I signed up for the bike course."

Angela rose to clear the dishes off the table. "Where does he live?"

"Toad Hollow."

This was the fanciful name given to a quiet court in the Tapley estate, the older part of town where Nate's parents, Jim and Leone, lived, and only a short walk away along the Valley Trail from Janice and Bob's house in Whistler Cay.

"I'll come, too, and visit...friends."

At least, she *hoped* Leone would still regard her in a friendly light. When Angela had married Nate, Leone had been like a surrogate mother to her, and after raising three boys, Angela became the daughter Leone never had.

They set off—Angela on foot and Ricky on his bike. White clouds hung over the mountains, obscuring the peaks, but the valley was bathed in sunlight. This section of the Valley Trail bordered the Whistler golf course and Angela's gaze was drawn to a group of players teeing off. She should have thought to bring her clubs.

Ricky rode slowly at first, keeping pace with Angela until she waved him on ahead after extracting a promise that he be home by five o'clock. She was glad of a few minutes alone to prepare for meeting Leone. Maybe she shouldn't just drop in but Wednesday had always been Leone's day off from her job as a public-health nurse and Angela was counting on her being at home.

Angela strode briskly along, imagining all the things she would say to her mother-in-law—things she couldn't say to Nate.

I'm sorry I hurt everyone, Leone. Running away was the biggest mistake of my life....

Leone would embrace her warmly. *You'll always be a cherished member of the Wilde family. Nate never stopped loving you....*

Angela rounded a bend and encountered a middle-aged woman striding along in walking shorts and a royal-blue T-shirt. "Leone!"

After a moment of initial surprise Leone's green eyes hardened. Her face was flushed with exertion and perspiration dampened her short auburn hair. There was no welcoming smile on her round face.

"I was on my way to see you..." Angela's words died away as her idiotic fantasies turned to dust. Leone would offer no reassuring phrases or warm embraces. Angela had wounded this woman's son. Had hurt *her*. For the first time Angela wondered how much of her decision to stay away from Whistler for so long had been to avoid facing the consequences of her youthful actions. "I should have called first."

Leone expelled a forceful sigh. "You can walk with me if you want."

Angela lengthened her stride to keep up with the older woman. "You're looking well."

"I'm still trying to work off the five pounds I gained during the Caribbean cruise Jim and I took last Christmas." She cast a sideways glance at Angela. "I was shocked when Nate told me you were back in town. What happened all those years ago? Why didn't we ever hear from you?"

"I sent a Christmas card the first year—"

"With no return address!"

"I'm sorry," Angela said quietly. "I figured no one would want to contact me after I ran out like that. I never meant to hurt anyone."

"I thought you and I were close," Leone reproached her. "If you needed someone to talk to, you could have come to me."

Angela gave Leone a troubled smile. "Nate is your son. You would have sided with him."

Leone was silent a moment. "Possibly, but I

would have understood. Sometimes Nate lets his pride get in the way of his good sense. I had no idea you two were having problems.''

A bicycle bell tinkled behind them and they moved to one side of the path to allow a pair of cyclists past. Angela was glad of the chance to collect her thoughts instead of blurting out the real reason she'd run away—her pregnancy.

''Maybe I should have come to you. You might have been able to give me advice on how to cope with being a cycling widow,'' Angela said instead. ''I know Nate's made a success out of his biking, but back then it seemed as though the sport was more important to him than our marriage.''

''Anyone who loves Nate has to accept that cycling will always be a major part of his life. Don't begrudge him his passion, Angela.''

While Angela was trying to think of an ungrudging response, Leone went on. ''So after all this time you've come home to get a divorce.''

''Did Nate tell you that?'' Angela felt her heart sink to the bottom of her stomach. Had she been wrong in thinking that the gleam in Nate's eye as she'd signed up for his bike course meant he wasn't indifferent?

''No, Aidan did. News travels quickly among the Wildes. But don't worry,'' Leone added, misinterpreting her expression. ''We don't spread gossip outside the family. Too much of that goes on in this valley as it is.''

''Nate and I are…'' Her words trailed away as she tried to figure out exactly *what* they were to each other and ended up repeating what she'd said to Nate. ''We're not enemies.'' It seemed a poor alternative to happily married.

They came to the railroad crossing and Leone paused to glance down the empty track. ''It's a blessing you didn't have children although I doubt Nate would agree.''

Angela gave her a sharp glance. Leone was a nurse. Had she suspected her daughter-in-law had been pregnant when she'd fled? Perhaps not. Leone's face gave no hint her remarks might refer to actual events. Angela should have relaxed but instead she felt even more troubled and again experienced an urge to confide in Leone. Until she recalled Leone's own words. *News spreads quickly among the Wildes.* This was one piece of news she had to tell Nate in her own time. *Which would be never.*

Trees had given way to bushes and through gaps Angela could see the gentle currents of the River of Golden Dreams. River of *Lost* Dreams was more apt.

Her steps slowed. Leone's eyebrows raised questioningly. ''I…I think I'll turn back,'' Angela said. ''I should do some work this afternoon while Ricky's occupied at Tim's.''

''Suit yourself.'' Leone hesitated and Angela hoped she would unbend and give her a hug but the moment passed. ''Have a nice stay in Whistler.''

As though she was tourist. ''Thanks. I will.''

''SQUIRT THE LUBRICANT BETWEEN the sprockets, Ricky—not too much,'' Nate admonished. ''Wipe the excess off the paintwork.''

They'd ridden the chairlift with their bikes—a lesson in itself—to the mountain bike training area on a plateau partway up Whistler Mountain. Nate strode among the group of eight youngsters signed up for his course giving instructions on basic maintenance. He paused beside Tim, a red-haired freckle-faced sprite. ''Try using the smaller wrench to tighten that nut.''

Nate went over all their names again, glancing at each in turn to commit them to memory. Besides Ricky and his friend Tim, there were Sean and Lee, two twelve-year-old boys from Squamish whose fees he'd waived because they were from disadvantaged homes. Cocky and at times belligerent, they'd been in trouble for minor offenses. Nate expected they'd settle down by the end of the course; these kids usually did once they got interested in something besides getting into trouble. Lisa and Jill were eleven-year-old best friends who dressed identically, right down to their puka beads and pink-corduroy overall shorts. Eleven-year-old David and his younger brother Mark were stocky and fair-haired, earnestly taking in every word Nate said.

And then there was Angela.

With her glossy hair and sleek figure she looked delectable in Lycra shorts and shirt. When she'd realized she had to hunker down and actually work on her borrowed bike she'd gone inside the ski hut and come out with sheets of paper towel. These she'd laid on the ground to kneel on.

"You're going to have to get over your fear of dirt if you're going to ride off-road," he said, squatting beside her.

"I lived the first half of my life battling dirt, whether it was in that awful trailer I grew up in or other people's messes I was paid to clean," she replied. "Now I live in a brand-new apartment. My clothes are clean. My hair is clean. My fingernails are clean. *Nothing* will induce me to go back to being dirty. Not even you."

"We'll see." He shifted his weight, one leg bent beneath him, his arm resting on his upright knee. "I'm surprised you're going through with this. The day you came down to the bike shop I was just baiting you.''

"I know. You always did when we were together." She paused, greasy rag pinched between two fingers, to appraise him. "Now that we're apart I wonder why you bother."

"You make it so much fun."

"Well, knock it off." She nudged him with an elbow, unbalancing him.

Nate righted himself with a smile he quickly wiped from his face. How was it he could be so angry with her on some levels yet still enjoy her company?

"Ricky is thrilled that I'm taking the course," she went on. "I overheard him bragging to Tim that his aunt would be riding, too. Last night he was really sweet, telling me all the hazards I might run into and how to get around them. Frankly, he gave me nightmares with all his talk about doing 'endos.' Are those what I think they are?"

"Flipping end over end, or in other words, falling headfirst off the bike over the handlebars? Yep. So why *are* you going through with it?"

She shrugged, as if she couldn't quite understand it herself. "I don't want to let him down."

"That's as good a reason as any. By the end of the course you'll be doing it because you love it."

"Huh!" she said. "Don't bet on that."

When they'd completed a half hour of basic maintenance, Nate took them over to the training course, a series of small hills, obstacles and teeter-totters which were perfect for teaching the kids to develop balance and technique. Last night's downpour had left puddles in several locations and low-lying sections of the track had turned to mud.

"Today I just want you to get a feel for off-road conditions," Nate told the class when they'd lined up, ready to start. "Try to avoid mud. Your mothers will thank you and your bikes will thank you."

"When are we going to do single track?" Sean demanded loudly. "I wanna get airborne."

"By the end of the course you'll be flying over moguls and navigating deer trails," Nate told them. "Before you tackle anything like that, you need to build your skills and stamina. Today you'll learn to ride in the ready position, as in ready for anything. Keep your butt off the seat and your arms and legs loose, letting your knees and elbows act as shock absorbers. Sean and Lee, you two can lead off but no hotdogging."

The older boys shot forward with the girls close behind. Gradually the class strung out in a line with Sean way in front and Angela trailing behind. Nate rode back and forth along the trail, encouraging his students and offering tips on when to change gears and how to brake safely in loose dirt.

He noticed Angela toiling grim-faced up a slope and slowed his pace to accompany her. "Drop down a gear and you'll find pedaling easier. No, the other lever. Push it the opposite direction—" He winced at the clashing metallic sound of gears being ground. "You're supposed to stop pedaling before you change gears. Haven't you ridden a bike before?"

"Not since I was twelve. My old Raleigh had one speed—slow." She made another attempt but with no forward impetus her bike stopped dead, wobbled and fell over. She jammed a foot out but the chain scraped her calf, leaving a long red welt on smooth shapely legs that likely hadn't seen a scratch or a bruise in years. She struggled to right the bicycle, swearing under her breath.

"Now, now," Nate chastised as he backtracked around her. "Remember there are children present."

"They're all miles ahead." She glared at him. "Are you going to circle like a buzzard waiting to pick me off, or are you going to help me!"

Nate tried not to smirk and didn't quite succeed. "I'm afraid sitting on the bike and pedaling is something you have to do for yourself."

She growled something under her breath but he could tell she wasn't as angry as she was making out.

"Pardon?" he said. "I didn't quite catch that."

"Be quiet and let me concentrate. It isn't easy balancing on uneven ground. Why can't we ride on pavement to start?"

"Then it wouldn't be mountain biking, would it? If you're not up to it, you can still quit…"

"*I don't quit.* Instead of harassing me you should be up ahead, looking out for Ricky. That kid's liable to ride off a cliff just to see if he can do it."

"I can take a hint. Careful of those gears."

He surged ahead on the trail, counting helmets. Every child was upright and accounted for. The older boys were on their second lap with Ricky and Tim not far behind. "You're doing great, boys. When you've gone around twice wait by those logs where the ground levels out and we'll practice wheelies."

One by one the kids finished the course and came to sit on the logs, their bikes beside them, drinking from water bottles and chattering about the ride so far. Angela still hadn't joined them.

Nate rode back over the trail wondering how she could have gotten lost. The course was big enough that riders were occasionally out of sight but not so large she couldn't find her way to the end.

And then he saw her, smack in the middle of a boggy dip off-trail. The bike was stuck up to its axles and Angela was trying to push it out, her shorts and T-shirt thickly splattered with mud.

"What the hell are you doing?" Nate demanded.

She glanced up and pushed back her hair, streaking her cheek with grime in the process. "I mastered the gravel and was looking for more of a challenge."

"Bull," he said, laughing. "You were so far behind you were embarrassed at being beaten by a bunch of kids and decided to take a shortcut."

Planting muddy fists on her hips, she demanded, "Are you going to get me out of here, or what?"

He crossed his arms over his chest. "Give me one good reason why I should. You disobeyed my orders to stay on the trail."

"You can't just leave me here!"

"You, I could happily leave. My bike, I'm going to rescue." He swung a leg off the Balfa, popped out the kickstand then strode into the mud. "Stand back." Grasping the bike by the handlebars and saddle, he heaved it free.

He set the bike on the trail and went back to help her. Ignoring his extended hand she stalked to dry land with her chin in the air and her running shoes making a sucking noise with every dragging step.

Angela went to wipe mud off her cheek and noticed her hands were filthy. She rubbed them on her shorts and they came away dirtier. Gritting her teeth she tried using her shoulder to scrub her face but couldn't reach the spot.

Nate suppressed his laughter and moistened a clean rag from the pouch on the back of his bike with water from his drink bottle. "Brown really isn't your color," he said, handing her the damp rag.

"Thanks." She wiped her face, shuddering a little when she saw the mud that came off.

"You missed a spot." With his thumb he dabbed at a smudge near the corner of her mouth and she tilted her face so he could wipe it more easily. Their eyes met. The dirt, the trail, even the bikes faded out as the air between them crackled. He had to admit, they still had chemistry. But what good was chemistry if they weren't getting involved again?

"What's this Albert character like?" he said, dropping his hand. The question had been bugging him for a long time.

She went over the spot near her mouth he'd just cleaned. "I told you, it's finished."

"That doesn't answer my question."

"He's a nice man who was supportive when I needed a friend," she said.

That didn't sound like grand passion. Nate hated

to admit he felt relieved. "Then why did you leave *him?*"

"The relationship wasn't working for either of us anymore." She used the cloth to scrub at her fingers. "He's…older than me."

"How old?"

Avoiding his gaze, she said, "Fifty-two."

"Fifty-two!" Nate exploded. "My *father* is fifty-two. That's it, isn't it? You were looking for a father figure. Security."

"Don't be ridiculous." Her voice lacked conviction.

"Were you in love with this joker?"

"We were very fond of each other. There was mutual respect. Love is for teenagers."

That last statement didn't ring true; not for Angela. Despite the grinding hardship of her childhood she'd had a deeply romantic streak. Nate grasped her by the shoulders and drew her closer. "When did the passionate woman I married turn so cynical?"

Angela trembled beneath his hands. He watched her gaze travel from his eyes to his mouth. As he struggled to keep his own desires under control he realized she wanted him to kiss her, whether she would admit it, or not. Well, she would have to ask.

Instead, she drew back suddenly. "Passion doesn't equal love."

Nate snorted. "Did Albert know you didn't love him?"

"Of course. I was completely honest with him. He didn't love me, either. But he was good to me. He never hurt me."

"I never wanted to hurt you, Ange."

"I didn't want to hurt you, either. Nevertheless, we did." She spoke flippantly, as if the pain and loneliness he'd endured meant nothing.

"You ran away."

"You let me go."

When he made no reply to her counteraccusation, Angela glanced away again. If he didn't know better he would have thought she was trying to hold back tears. But Angela was too tough for tears. A moment later, his assessment was confirmed when she turned back to him, her blue eyes dry and fierce. "What do you want from me? *Anything?*"

Yes, he wanted something. He wanted to not compare every woman he met with her. He wanted to not imagine her in bed with other men. He wanted her to admit she was wrong to run away so his heartbreak wouldn't have been completely in vain.

But he couldn't say all that so he got back on

his bike. "The kids will be waiting to continue the lesson."

He rode ahead, glancing back over his shoulder to check on Angela. She was pedaling so slowly Nate could have walked faster but she wasn't giving up until she completed the ride.

His gaze veered west across the valley and beyond. Over the ocean the sky was clear and a balmy breeze was blowing in from the Pacific. Cloud patterns on the horizon promised continued fine weather ahead. Pity life wasn't so predictable, or so temperate.

When he'd asked her about filing for divorce, at first she'd said if, not when. *If.* A little word with big implications. But he wasn't sticking his neck out again, not without something more concrete to go on.

ANGELA HEATED UP two servings of frozen lasagna for dinner and because she knew kids should eat their vegetables, she popped some frozen French fries in the oven.

"You're a really good cook, Angela," Ricky said later, tucking in with gusto. "Mom hardly ever makes this kind of yummy stuff. She and Dad like stir-fries and vegetable soup." He made such a gruesome face, Angela had to laugh.

"Glad you like it, kiddo." Angela helped herself

to a small portion of lasagna. "I'd love to make stir-fry. I've just never taken the time to learn how."

The phone rang and Angela got up to answer it.

"Angela? It's Janice."

"Janice! Where are you?"

"Amsterdam. We're having a great time. The weather's perfect, the food is wonderful. We've seen the Van Gogh museum and today we're going on a canal boat ride."

"Do you want to talk to Ricky? He's just eating dinner."

"Let him finish. How are you doing?"

"I'm glad you called. Somewhat against my better judgment I signed Ricky up for Nate's mountain-bike course. Mountain biking can be dangerous, Janice. If you say no, I'll pull him out."

"Aside from the expense..."

"I'm giving it to Ricky as an early birthday present."

"Angela, *thank* you. You're too good to us. I wish there was some way I could repay you."

"It's nothing, really. Don't even think about it." Angela took the cordless phone and wandered into the living room.

"Then as long as Ricky wears padding and a helmet, I can't see why not. Nate's great with kids. Plus, you'll get a break from looking after Ricky."

"Not exactly. I signed up for the course, too."

"You're kidding! What are you up to? Is this a ploy to get Nate back? If so, I predict he'll crack in a week."

Angela groaned and threw herself into an armchair. "He's the most aggravating man I've ever known."

And the most exciting. But their confrontation on the bike track had brought home to her that she couldn't just ignore their unresolved issues and pick up where they'd left off even if she wanted to. What she didn't understand was why he hadn't kissed her when she was so sure he wanted to. That wasn't like the Nate she thought she knew.

Casually, she added, "It's odd Nate never hooked up with anyone else even though we both agreed years ago we could go out with other people. Has he had any serious relationships?"

"I'm always trying to give you the gossip on Nate but you barely listen to a word about the man."

"When I was three thousand miles away I didn't want to know who he was dating or be reminded of what I'd left behind."

"Nate doesn't exactly confide in me about his love life but I've seen him with quite a few women over the years," Janice said. "He's an attractive guy, Angela. You shouldn't have let him alone so long.''

''Never mind that. Who's the latest?''

''Kerry Martin, Tim's mom. Nate went out with her for over a year.''

''Kerry Martin. Wasn't she the girl in high school with horn-rim glasses and greasy braids?''

''That was then. Now she's got contact lenses, changed her shampoo and looks like a million bucks. She and her husband divorced a couple of years ago. After he moved out she turned their chalet into a bed-and-breakfast.''

''So is Nate still seeing her? He told me he didn't have a girlfriend.''

''According to my friend Phyllis, who cuts Kerry's hair, they called it quits by mutual agreement. Kerry was angling for a wedding ring and Nate wasn't free to commit.''

''Yet he didn't get in touch with me to ask for a divorce. Interesting. Although,'' she added hastily, ''that doesn't necessarily mean anything.''

''What would you like it to mean?'' Janice teased.

''Don't be annoying, little sister,'' Angela said. ''Anything else I should know?''

''I forgot to mention, there's a trunk full of your things in the garage Nate dropped off years ago. You might want to go through it.''

"I will. Hang on, Ricky's done. Give my love to Bob."

While Ricky chatted to his mom and dad, Angela finished her lasagna then went out to the garage. Behind the gardening tools and spare car parts was a stack of cardboard cartons full of Christmas decorations and Halloween costumes. On the bottom was the old steamer trunk Janice mentioned. Angela moved the boxes aside and dragged the trunk into a clear spot.

The latches were rusty but she managed to prize them up and lift the heavy lid. Inside were clothes—had she really worn that awful blouse?—books and a shoe box full of bundles of tissue paper. Curious, she started to unwrap them. Oh! Her eyes filled with tears. It was the set of china horses she'd collected as a girl.

One by one she pulled out the little bundles and unwrapped her precious figurines. There was the rearing black stallion, the gentle bay, the prancing chestnut, the palomino and her favorite, the dapple gray with the silver mane and tail. During their marriage Nate had teased her about her beloved horses. When she'd left she'd wanted to send for them but she'd been too embarrassed, and presumed Nate would have disposed of them as junk.

Instead, he'd wrapped them individually in tissue paper and stored them carefully. Gratefully she kissed the gray on the nose and tucked it back in its place.

Next she found a plastic bag full of brown-and-cream wool and the half-knit Nordic style sweater she'd started making in secret for Nate's birthday. Digging through the balls of wool she found the pattern and circular knitting needles. It seemed a shame to waste the effort that had already gone into the sweater; she might as well finish it for him. Tie up loose ends, so to speak.

Piling everything else back into the trunk she carried the shoe box and the sweater back to the house. She was arranging the little horses on the table, her back to the door into the hall when she heard the sound of the front door opening. ''Ricky?''

''No, me.'' Nate appeared in his bike shorts and shirt, his helmet tucked beneath his arm. ''Ricky let me in. I'll only stay a minute.''

Instinctively Angela spread her arms in front of the table where her horses stood. ''It's okay. Where *is* Ricky?''

''Out front, riding his bike. You should be practicing, too. It's important to master the basics before you get on a tech trail.''

''Oh, please. Do you realize how silly I feel attempting a maneuver called a 'wheelie'? Imagine what I'd look like cavorting on the street like a kid on my bike."

Nate's gaze traveled past her to the china horses with a faint smile. "Since when did you care what anyone thought of you?"

She felt her cheeks grow warm. "I was going through my old trunk. Thank you for saving these. It means a lot to me."

He shrugged, as though it was nothing. She pushed the bundle of knitting spilling from the plastic bag back inside and hung the bag over the back of the chair before he could ask what it was. "Do you want coffee?"

"No, thanks. I really can't stay. I only came to give you this." Nate ripped open the Velcro tab on his shorts pocket and removed a slightly bent card with a computer-generated color picture of balloons and streamers floating above clinking wineglasses. "My mother wants to invite you to her birthday party this Sunday. She said to apologize for the short notice. You can bring Ricky, if you want. There'll be other kids."

"I'd love to come," Angela said, accepting the card. "Did your mom mention I ran into her on the Valley Trail the other day?"

Nate nodded. "She seemed to think she wasn't very welcoming. She didn't want any hard feelings."

"I appreciate that."

The silence grew a little awkward. Nate glanced out the window. The sun had gone below the mountains and the luminous blue sky was fading to dusk. "I'd better go. It'll be dark soon."

"Nate?" she said, and he paused in the doorway. "You don't have a problem with me coming to the party, do you?"

He looked at her strangely. "You're my mother's guest. She can invite whomever she wants." He strapped on his helmet and touched his fingers to it in salute.

After he left, Angela went to the bedroom and lifted the top tray off the scarlet lacquered jewelry box she'd bought in Vancouver's Chinatown before she'd moved to Toronto. Nestled in a velvet slot was a plain band of gold she'd worn so briefly it was still shiny and unscratched. Inscribed on the inner surface were the words Nate had spoken in his vows. *Yours until the mountains crumble to the sea.*

Forever just wasn't what it used to be.

CHAPTER FOUR

At closing time on Friday Nate flipped the Open sign on his shop door over to Closed and announced to the half-dozen biking enthusiasts who regularly hung out after hours, "Beer time."

"Way ahead of you," said Kevin, already handing out cans from the bar fridge at the back of the workshop.

Nate accepted a cold beer and pulled off the tab, grateful for the welcome distraction from his recent habit of spending the evenings prowling about his house, brooding over Angela. He kept telling himself he was glad she was filing for divorce. Best for both of them. The only sensible course of action, really. Then he'd think of the sparkle in her eye and the way her smile lit her face and he'd get all confused again.

Tonight the gang was buzzing with talk of the Gravity Festival coming up at the end of the month, a week-long series of mountain-biking events and races. Everyone present was taking part in one or several races, from Chris's first-time entry in the free-ride event to Rachel leading a ladies-only group ride. Everyone was participating, that is, except Nate.

"C'mon, Nate. Why don't you enter the downhill this year?" Kevin asked. "All the guys from Denver and Kamloops will be there. Charlie Wenham is coming over from Australia just for the occasion. It'll be a hoot."

Nate took a long pull on his beer, tempted. The Gravity Fest downhill was the only major race he'd never won. Reluctantly he shook his head. "You know I don't compete these days. The store takes all my time, especially now that we're expanding to Vancouver."

"All the more reason to enter one last race before you're completely tied up," Kevin insisted.

"Oh, I meant to tell you, Nate," Rachel said from a camp chair wedged between a row of bikes and the tire display. "The Children's Hospital Society contacted us. They're looking for people to race during the Gravity Festival for charity. You know, collect sponsors and donate the money. They specifically asked about you."

"Probably because I've helped them out in the past. But you have to be in constant training to race," Nate said. "The competition's fierce."

"It doesn't matter if you don't win if it's for a good cause," Rachel countered.

A chorus of agreement met this statement. Nate didn't bother pointing out he wasn't psychologically capable of riding without the aim of winning.

"No one's suggesting you go back on the circuit," Chris added persuasively. "Just one more race. What can it hurt?"

"You put the rest of us to shame, man. A few weeks hard riding and you'll be in peak form," scoffed Kevin. "Why not go for it?"

"Think of the kids," Rachel reminded him.

Nate met her gaze and shook his head when she grinned, knowing she'd got to him. Deep down he missed racing. For a moment he was torn, wondering what Angela would think after he'd told her he'd quit. It was only one race, he reasoned. Anyway, she didn't own him.

"What the hell," he said, throwing his hands in the air. "Where do I sign up?"

"Entry forms are on the cash desk," Rachel informed him triumphantly over the general noise of approbation which greeted his announcement.

"This calls for another beer," Chris suggested.

"Not for me, thanks," Nate said, glancing at his watch. "I'm heading to Vancouver early tomorrow. My cousin Marc is coming in on a flight and I'm picking him up."

"Will you have time to meet with the contractor about the renovations on the new store?" Rachel asked, reverting to her role as assistant manager. "We've got stock ordered and we need a firm completion date."

Nate calculated how much time he'd have before Marc's flight got in and decided he could squeeze in the meeting before he picked up Marc.

"I could meet with the contractor if you'd like," Rachel suggested when he didn't answer right away. "I'm going to Vancouver tomorrow anyway to see my boyfriend."

"Why don't we both talk to him?" Nate replied. "I'll set up a time and give you a call first thing in the morning. And you know when I say first thing, I mean—"

"—the crack of dawn." Rachel groaned and nodded.

Nate gave her shoulder a squeeze. "I'll appreciate your input." He lifted a hand to the rest of the group. "Catch you all later."

The next day Nate was on the road early for his meeting with the contractor. Afterward he left Rachel to sort out the details, picked Marc up from the airport and they headed back to Whistler in Nate's black Jeep Cherokee.

"I can't wait to shower and shave," Marc said, rubbing a hand across his deeply tanned jaw where two days of stubble had sprouted. His dark blond hair lay uncharacteristically flat and his faded denim jacket and khaki combat pants had the rumpled look of being slept in.

"You'll be doing us all a favor." Nate wrinkled his nose in Marc's direction, dodging when Marc threw him a jabbing punch to the arm.

"I hear Angela's back in town," Marc said as they exited Vancouver through a thickly forested section of Stanley Park.

Nate cast his cousin a surprised glance. "Your news sources in Pakistan are better than I thought."

Marc laughed. "My 'source' is Leone. She told me when I called to tell her which flight I was coming in on. Is it true Angela wants a divorce?"

"So she says." In a few words Nate recapped the previous morning in his bike shop and casually, almost as an afterthought, asked Marc's opinion of the significance of Angela's use of the word *if*.

Traffic slowed as they started across the suspension bridge to the north shore. "Sounds to me like a Freudian slip," Marc said finally. "If she was serious about a divorce she would have gone ahead and filed and *then* told you about it."

"I hadn't thought of that," Nate lied. "But I'm sure she's at least considering it."

Marc turned his piercing blue gaze on him. "The question is, what do *you* want?"

Nate was silent. Less than a week ago he'd thought he'd known. Now he wasn't so sure.

"Have you talked over whatever went wrong in the past?" Marc added when Nate still didn't speak. "Maybe you two can work things out."

"We've talked some, but nothing's been resolved. As far as I can figure out she blames our breakup all on me and my bikes. Back when we were living together she wanted me to give up cycling to prove my love for her. Nothing else would convince her. And believe me, I tried everything."

"She was jealous of your outside interests. Maybe a little insecure."

"Insecure—Angela? The woman has a hide like a rhino. She hasn't changed."

"I always liked Angela," Marc mused. "You wouldn't want her to change too much."

"To tell you the truth, we weren't married long enough to really know each other well. But we have this…I don't know…*connection*. A spark that just won't die regardless of the years or the distance." He lifted his shoulders then let them fall. "You can't build a marriage on a spark. Anyway, she's not interested in trying."

"Will I get a chance to see her while I'm here?"

"Tomorrow at Mom's party."

Marc raised his eyebrows at that. "Leone invited her? I got the impression she wasn't too happy about Angela turning up. She's worried you'll get hurt again.''

''I can take care of myself.'' A moment later Nate admitted reluctantly, ''*I* asked Mom to invite Angela.''

And he'd been so annoyed with himself for doing so that he'd immediately rung Kerry and asked her out to dinner the evening following the party. Kerry had seemed surprised but pleased and had agreed readily.

Marc chuckled all the way to the turnoff to Whistler. ''If you want her back—''

''I don't.''

''But clearly you want *something*,'' Marc insisted.

Both hands gripping the steering wheel, Nate slowed for a sharp corner around a sheer rock face on the narrow road. ''I want her to admit she was wrong to leave, that she's sorry she did. And that we had something good and she destroyed it.''

ANGELA WALKED PAST a long line of cars parked down the block from the log home Jim Wilde had built over thirty years ago. Douglas fir trees towered over the peaked roof and split firewood was stacked along the fence beside the driveway. Wooden barrels either side of the front steps were planted with red and white geraniums.

With Ricky at her side, Angela rang the bell, her shoulders straight, her grip firm on a small gift-wrapped box. In spite of the invitation she felt uncertain of her reception.

Jim flung back the door, took one look at her and opened his arms to draw her into his bearlike embrace, as familiar and longed for as if he were her own father and she the prodigal daughter. "Welcome home, Angela."

"It's wonderful to see you again." Angela had to fight the sudden urge to bury her face in Jim's shirt and cry at his warm reception. When she drew back blinking, she touched her fingertips to the moist skin below her eyes, hoping her mascara hadn't smudged.

"Hi there, Ricky," Jim said, ruffling the boy's hair. "The other kids are in the backyard playing on the trampoline. Just go down the hall, through the family room and out the sliding doors."

Ricky ran off. Jim and Angela followed more slowly, past the hall table where fresh flowers gave off a sweet scent and the living room with its huge stone fireplace rising to a cathedral ceiling. There a few people were clustered around a side table with photographs, and a teenage girl was picking out notes on the baby grand piano in the corner. From deeper in the house the burble of conversation and laughter rose above the muted clink of glass and china.

"I don't know what that son of mine was thinking when he let you go," Jim said, as they headed toward the family room at the back. "I hope he's gained the sense to try to win you back."

Jim's once-black hair was a little grayer through the temples than Angela remembered yet he was still fit and vital. *This was how Nate would look when he was older.*

"I...I'm afraid I'm only here temporarily."

"You're not serious about this divorce nonsense, I hope. You two better sit down and talk things out."

"I wish it were that easy."

"Marriage *isn't* always easy. You have to work at it. But never mind that now. Aidan's here, and Marc flew in for a few days. Can I get you a drink? I've made my famous planter's punch."

"Thanks. That would be great." She glanced around for her mother-in-law. "Where's Leone? I'd like to give her her birthday gift."

"She's probably in the kitchen. I told her we should have the party catered but she wouldn't hear of it. Had to make everything herself, with help from Nate's friend, Kerry."

Angela sniffed the savory aromas coming from

the kitchen appreciatively. "Whatever they've made smells delicious."

The open-concept kitchen and family room was crowded with guests who spilled through open sliding-glass doors onto the patio. Platters of food were laid out on the dining table, buffet style, and rows of crystal wineglasses were lined up alongside Leone's best china plates.

"Leone!" Jim called to his wife who was taking a tray of hot appetizers out of the oven. "Look who's here." He patted Angela's arm and moved away toward the buffet table. "I'll get you that punch."

Angela threaded her way through to the kitchen to present her gift. "Happy birthday, Leone."

"Thank you, my dear." Leone smiled briefly and held her cheek out for Angela to kiss. Her eyes were guarded, not quite meeting Angela's as she unwrapped the silver foil. "French lavender soap, my favorite. How thoughtful."

"I'm glad you like it." Angela smiled stiffly, wishing they could get past this awkwardness. "Can I help you with anything?"

"Thank you, no. Kerry and I have everything under control." Leone set the soap aside and went back to transferring tiny choux pastries from the baking tray to a serving dish.

Kerry again. Angela smiled brightly. "In that case, I'll just go...mingle. Talk to you later!"

She left the kitchen, glancing outside for Ricky. He was with Tim and some other children bouncing on the trampoline, watched over by an exuberant Irish setter. Satisfied Ricky was keeping out of trouble, she scanned the room. Amid the blur of faces, her gaze homed in on Nate.

He was standing in the doorway to the patio, deep in conversation with a woman with lustrous chestnut hair. That must be Kerry Martin. A fierce wave of jealousy swept through Angela. Nate was *her* man, and this was *her* territory.

As though aware of her watching him, Nate glanced up, saw Angela and nodded before turning back to Kerry.

His cool acknowledgment, unaccompanied by any invitation to join them, made her cheeks burn. Then Leone, handing around a tray of appetizers, paused to speak to Nate and Kerry. She squeezed Kerry's arm and laughed warmly at something the younger woman said, completing Angela's humiliation. During her long absence Kerry had become a familiar and welcome guest in the Wilde family home. Like one of the family.

Angela felt an arm curl around her shoulder followed by a cool glass being pressed into her hand and turned to see Nate's cousin, Marc.

"Jim said to give you this." Marc's smile was boyish and easygoing but his eyes seemed too old for his twenty-eight years, as if he'd already seen more than a lifetime of horror and sorrow.

"Marc!" She threw her free arm around his neck in a hug. "I'm so glad I happened to be in Whistler for one of your flying visits."

"I'm the lucky one." He stepped back to give her a friendly wolf whistle and, unconsciously echoing his uncle, added, "What was Nate thinking to let you go?"

"He wasn't thinking, isn't it obvious?" she said lightly, sipping Jim's potent fruit juice and rum punch.

"Ah, now if you'd been *my* wife…" Marc's slow smile filled in the rest.

Marc flirted as automatically and as thoughtlessly as he breathed, but his open admiration salved her bruised ego.

"You'd have left me to go cover some war," she said, smiling. She loved Marc like a brother but she pitied any woman who fell in love with the restless wanderer. "Tell me what you've been doing since I saw you last."

Marc ran a hand through his sun-bleached hair and the braided circle of leather around his wrist slid up his forearm. "Just lately I've been following a camel caravan into the tribal areas of Pakistan in search of members of al-Qaeda.''

As Marc filled her in on his travels, other people joined them, drawn by tales of sniper fire and mortar blasts. What with Marc's attention being claimed by others and the mellowing effect of Jim's punch, Angela's gaze kept drifting toward Nate. Once or twice his eyes met hers and she experienced a jolt to her midriff, as though a switch had been flipped on an electromagnet. Had he felt it, too?

The next time she looked, Kerry was talking to someone else and Nate was taking the tray from Leone's hands, apparently chastising her good-naturedly for working at her own party. Angela watched the interplay of humor and affection between Nate and his mother. Good sons made good husbands. Did that mean the fault for their failed marriage lay with her?

Her fingers tightened on her empty glass, and she turned away, meaning to find herself another drink, only to bump into Aidan Wilde.

''Aidan, hi. It's good to see you.'' When she'd known him he'd been as warm and open as the other Wilde boys. Now she would have liked to give him a sisterly hug but his reserve was like a force field keeping her at bay. ''I'm so sorry about Charmaine. How are you?''

"I'm fine, thanks." His gaze flickered away.

Either he wasn't fine or he was tired of people trying to console him. "I should have written to you at the time, but…" But she'd just started seeing Albert and felt awkward contacting Nate's family.

"Never mind. Now that you're back in town it's almost like old times." His smile gained warmth as he deflected the conversation away from himself. "We've all missed you." He paused. "Nate's missed you."

"Really?" Her gaze went to Nate who'd been waylaid by two pretty teenagers while circulating with the appetizer tray. Angela gave Aidan a rueful smile. "I'm sure he hasn't been lonely."

"Many have tried but no one has claimed his heart." Aidan's gaze searched her face. "Is there any chance you still have feelings for him?"

Heat flooded her cheeks. She had plenty of feelings about Nate but none she wanted to share with his brother and closest confidant. She was saved from answering when a little girl ran up to Aidan and clutched his leg. She stared up at Angela with round blue eyes, a perfect, doll-like version of Aidan's beautiful late wife.

"This must be…" Angela racked her brains, trying to remember the name of Aidan's daughter.

"Emily." He helped her out, stroking the girl's long blond hair. "Say hello to Angela, Em."

"Hello," Emily whispered. She turned her face up to her father and lisped, "Can I have a soda, Daddy?"

"Sure thing, honey. What are you drinking, Angela?"

"Your dad's punch, but I'd forgotten how deadly it was. I think I'd better switch to mineral water." Angela went with them to the table and helped herself.

Aidan smiled apologetically in farewell as he moved away. "I'm going to get Emily some food. I'll catch up with you again later."

She watched him shepherd his daughter around the table, a protective hand hovering over her shoulders. Aidan made a great dad but she sensed he and Emily were almost too self-contained. Then she spied an old acquaintance and was about to go say hello when a voice spoke behind her.

"Crab puff?" Nate proffered the nearly empty tray. "I saved the last one for you."

"Thanks. I was wondering when you'd get around to me." She took the crab puff and bit into it, savoring the creamy curry flavor. "I've enjoyed seeing your parents and Aidan and Marc again. Aside from your mom your family has been very welcoming considering…'' Her words trailed away.

''We're getting a divorce?'' Nate supplied dryly. ''*You're* getting the divorce. I'm being dragged along for the ride.''

''Would you rather we stayed married?'' The hand holding the crab puff stopped halfway to her mouth as she waited for his answer.

His gaze was level and cool. ''Do I have a choice?''

He was going to drive her crazy with these enigmatic comments. ''Was that Kerry Martin you were talking to?'' she asked.

''Yes. I'm surprised you haven't met her yet given that Ricky and Tim play together all the time.''

''The boys ride their bikes to each other's houses.''

''I'll introduce you.'' Before she could stop him, Nate waved to Kerry from across the room and she made her way toward them.

''You must be Angela,'' Kerry said, holding out her hand with a friendly smile. ''I remember you from high school but you look so different now. I love your dress.''

''Thanks. It's nice to see you again.''

Kerry put a hand on Nate's arm and spoke to him. ''Sorry I abandoned you earlier. Old Mr.

Garrity was standing all by himself.'' To Angela, she explained, ''The poor man is lost since his wife passed away.''

''How sad, but it's nice of you to look after him.'' It would have been easier if she was able to dislike Kerry but that didn't seem likely. ''Ricky and Tim are having a great time in Nate's mountain bike course.''

''I hear you're taking the course, too,'' Kerry replied. ''When Ricky's over at our house he brags about how well you're doing.''

''He's exaggerating. I'm hopeless.''

''You'll be fine,'' Kerry said warmly. ''Nate taught even me to bunny hop. It's so much fun.''

''Oh, yeah, bunny hopping's the best,'' Angela lied shamelessly. *What in the world was bunny hopping?*

Nate snorted and Angela glared at him. ''Excuse me.'' He covered his mouth. ''My drink went down the wrong way.''

''Are you okay?'' Kerry patted him on the back then rubbed in circles, turning her ministrations into a caress. Then to Angela's relief Kerry glanced at her watch. ''I've got to go. I've got guests arriving this afternoon and I have to be there to greet them. It was nice to see you, Angela. Let's get together soon for coffee.'' Angela nodded, and

Kerry transferred her warm smile to Nate. "I'll see you tomorrow night for dinner."

"I'll pick you up around seven."

"Wonderful." Kerry turned to Angela. "You don't mind, do you? Nate told me you were formalizing your situation."

"Oh, no, I don't mind." Then she had to watch while Kerry planted a kiss right on Nate's mouth and then drew back, holding his gaze.

Angela's smile became fixed. Theoretically she had no right to care that her soon-to-be-ex-husband was having dinner with another woman. As far as Kerry or anyone knew she wasn't in love with him anymore.

After Kerry left, Nate turned to Angela. "I'm pleased you already know how to bunny hop," he said blandly. "Maybe you can give the class some pointers."

Angela resisted the urge to punch him. "You know darn well I don't know how to do it, or even what it is!"

"Jumping over logs."

"*On a bike?* Is that possible?"

"You've seen me do it."

Oh, heck. She had, too, once when she'd watched him in a free-ride competition. Her heart had been in her mouth the entire time. "You know, for someone who isn't a girlfriend, Kerry does an awfully good imitation.''

''I don't have a *steady* girlfriend but Kerry and I go out occasionally.'' He regarded her thoughtfully. ''You wouldn't be jealous, by any chance?''

''Me, jealous? Of course not.'' She wondered if dating occasionally meant sleeping together occasionally, too. ''Once we're divorced you'd be able to marry her.''

Nate's gaze narrowed. ''And you wouldn't mind?''

Angela lifted her shoulders carelessly, at least she hoped that's how it appeared. ''She's pretty and she's nice. You could do worse.''

''Maybe.'' Nate leaned closer. ''You know that thing that happens when our eyes meet across the room?'' he said in a low voice that reached right down into the pit of her stomach. ''You and I still have chemistry.''

He *wasn't* indifferent. And yet, he was going out with Kerry. Angela said dryly, ''If I'd known chemistry was going to figure so importantly in my life I'd have paid more attention in science class.''

Nate just grinned, the twinkle in his dark eyes sending her stomach into free fall.

''I'd better get going, too,'' she added, almost stumbling over her own feet in her effort to back away. She went in search of Ricky and found he'd taken his shoes off to jump on the trampoline and was now wiping blood from a stubbed toe onto the grass. She got him a Band-Aid, said goodbye to Leone and Jim and started on the short walk home.

She had to admit, she was seriously confused. Nate's combination of seductive charm and ego-crushing indifference was enough to make any woman crazy.

And crazy for him.

Or could it simply be that Kerry had aroused her competitive spirit? If Kerry could bunny hop for Nate, so would Angela.

CHAPTER FIVE

ADVANTAGE OF BACHELORHOOD Number 151: Dating gorgeous babes.

The only trouble was, last night Nate had dated the *wrong* gorgeous babe. Plus he'd felt like a heel when he'd had to subtly let Kerry know he'd asked her out as a friend, not because he wanted to renew their romance.

Nate circled the level dirt lot at the mountain bike training area on his Balfa while his band of beginners donned helmets and mounted their bikes. Angela was last, as usual. Her legs straddling the crossbar, she fiddled with the catch on her helmet strap and glared at him every time he circled past.

"'Morning, Sunshine. We're waiting for you."

"I can't do up this darn strap," she growled.

"Let me take a look." Nate dismounted, knocked out the kickstand with his heel and walked over to Angela. Pushing her hands out of the way, he inspected the strap. "No wonder. You've got it twisted inside out." He tried to turn it back on itself and accidentally brushed the soft skin beneath her jaw. Suddenly he was all thumbs. "What have you done to this?" he muttered, getting it more tangled.

"How was your dinner with Kerry?" Angela's warm breath on his wrists set his nerve endings to tingling.

"Wonderful." Sensing her gaze, he lifted his eyes to hers and felt the mountain tilt. In cycling, forward momentum was essential to staying upright and balanced; if he kept talking he just might not crash and burn under the force of Angela's fiery blue eyes. "She's a fantastic cook," he went on. "Her blueberry muffins are out of this world. She gets repeat business on the basis of them alone."

"I'll just bet she does," Angela said dryly.

The fastener clicked into place and he stepped back, breathing again. "That should do it."

Angela's fingertips touched the spot on her neck where his had rested, then curled into her palm. "So she made dinner for you at her house last night?"

"No, we went out to eat. But I've been to her place lots of times."

"She probably makes a great breakfast." Angela was watching him closely.

"Oh, she does. In fact, she's giving a brunch in a couple of weeks. You're invited." He crouched to check a small nut on her front wheel. It wiggled beneath his fingers. "Hand me a wrench."

Angela twisted around to dig through the tool pouch behind her saddle. "Why would she want me?"

"Kerry's not the type to feel threatened by other women—"

"And I am? Is that what you're saying?" She turned back to him, brandishing a three-inch wrench.

Nate chuckled. "If you're going to brain me, at least use something that will do some damage." He took the wrench from her and tightened the loose nut. Angela might be aggravating but, by God, he enjoyed getting a rise out of her. "I wouldn't turn the invitation down. Kerry's muffins really are delicious." He closed his eyes and affected a dreamy expression.

Angela got off the bike and took a step toward him, chin jutted forward. "Is that what she cooked for breakfast this morning?"

"Why? Are you interested in graduating beyond Pop-Tarts and cold pizza?" He moved back a pace, leading her on. This was more fun than a twenty-foot drop. "If you ask her nicely, I'm sure she'd give you the recipe."

Angela backed him up against a storage shed, one step away from full frontal contact. "Janice said you and Kerry stopped seeing each other months ago. Are you back together again?"

Kiss her, a voice inside him urged. "I explained—"

"Never mind what you said." She lifted her face, the better to level her glittering blue gaze at him. A rosy flush filled her cheeks. "Are you back together?" she repeated. "Or do you just sleep with her once in a while?"

He would swear Angela was enjoying their sparring as much as he was, but he couldn't let her think Kerry went in for casual sex. "Who said I was sleeping with her?"

She blinked, taken aback. "You mean you didn't stay over at her house last night? But you said—"

"I said nothing. You jumped to conclusions."

"You let me think—! Oh, you." She paced a few steps away then circled back, eyes gleaming, for a fresh attack. "So, you spent the night alone after a platonic evening with your ex-girlfriend. Now you're trading insults with your ex-wife. Your love life really sucks, Wilde."

Leaning in close, he whispered, "Now that you're back maybe it'll improve."

"You wish." She placed both hands flat on his chest as if to push him away but instead, her fingers splayed over his chest, pressing lightly, until her heat penetrated the thin fabric of his bike shirt.

When his gaze met hers, the gleam in her eyes intensified. *Kiss her,* the inner voice urged again. His hands gravitated to her waist, thumbs settling on the peaks of her hipbones as if they'd been apart ten minutes rather than ten years. His mouth dried and his breath came short and fast. *Kiss her.*

A wolf whistle broke the taut silence, followed by jeers and cheers from Sean and Lee. "Go for it, man! Woo hoo!"

Ricky rounded on Sean, saying something short and sharp in his aunt's defense and gave the taller boy a shove that almost knocked him and his bike over.

Nate swore under his breath and snatched his hands away from Angela. What was he thinking, fooling around like this in front of the kids? That was the story of his life with Angela; when they got physical his brains went south.

"Knock it off, guys. We'll show no disrespect toward the ladies." He strode over to the knot of kids. "Who wants to learn to bunny hop?" That elicited a different kind of cheer from the group and the incident with him and Angela was quickly forgotten.

Or maybe not by everyone. From the corner of his eye he watched Angela in earnest conversation with Ricky. She was shaking her head. *No,* he suspected she was saying, *nothing's going on between me and Nate.* Like hell.

He got on his Balfa and circled back to Angela and Ricky, glancing from one to the other. "Everything okay?" he asked Angela, and she nodded.

"Off you go, dude," he said to Ricky, and the boy obediently cycled off to join the others.

"How do you do that?" Angela demanded.

"I'm not afraid of him." Her eyes widened but before she could protest, he asked, "Have you told him we're married?"

"No. I told you I wasn't going to. He'd only be confused."

"That would make two of us." Nate pushed off and rode ahead of the group to a log of about four inches diameter.

He raised his voice so everyone could hear. "When you're riding single track and come across a fallen log, you don't want to be a weenie who has to dismount and carry your bike over. You want to ride right up to the log, bring up your front wheel and float over that sucker. I hope you've all been practicing your wheelies because they're the basis of the bunny hop. Getting the wheel in the air isn't enough—forward projection is critical. Envision your bike smoothly lifting off and soaring over the log or rock or whatever obstacle is in your path. Ideally your rear wheel should touch down first, followed by your front wheel.''

''Watch while I demonstrate.'' He cycled a few yards away then turned to ride swiftly back, talking as he went. ''Build speed as you approach the obstacle…bring your weight down hard on the pedals, crankshafts parallel. This compresses the tires and acts as a springboard…'' He threw his weight onto the pedals. ''Then shift your weight back, lift up on the handlebars, hold on tight…and you're flying and styling.'' His front wheel rose into the air and the bike sailed over the log. He landed effortlessly on the other side, the rear wheel skimming the ground a fraction of a second before the front.

''Who wants to go first?'' He glanced down the line of eager faces as a chorus of ''*Me*s'' greeted his question. All, that is, except for Angela, whose drawn face was almost as pale as her knuckles. ''Angela. Off you go.''

''Pick someone else,'' she said quickly. ''I don't mind waiting.''

''The longer you delay, the harder it'll be. Honestly.''

He wasn't trying to embarrass her but he knew unless he forced her, she was capable of stalling indefinitely. If she didn't master the basics she'd be left behind when they came to the hard stuff. "Come on."

She shook her head. Sean and Lee sniggered.

"You can do it, Aunt Angela," Ricky urged, his cheeks flaming. "I know you can."

Ricky shamed her into trying. She cycled far enough away from the log to get a good run at it and paused to wipe her hands on her shorts. Then, her mouth set in grim determination, she rode toward the log.

"Faster," Nate called. "Keep your butt off the seat in the ready position, legs flexed, arms loose." Dammit, she was so tight she was bound to do a face plant. "Stand on those crankshafts. *Now*. And lift."

Her timing was way off. She reached the log and her bike came to a dead stop, like a horse balking at a jump. Angela flew forward over the handlebars to land in an awkward sprawl on the other side of the log.

Nate hopped off his bike and ran over to her. She came up spitting dirt, her knee bleeding.

"Why are you making me do this?" she demanded. "I'm not ready."

His swift, detached inspection for sprains or broken bones yielded nothing. "You'll be fine. Get up, brush yourself off and try again."

"No!" she said in a furious undertone, her eyes flashing.

He held her by the shoulders and spoke in a firm undertone. "Do you want Sean and Lee to think they're smarter and braver than a grown woman?"

"Why should I care what those little brats think?"

"You care what Ricky thinks."

She went silent, eyes downcast.

"Get back on the horse, Ange." He spoke more gently and his grip relaxed, turning perilously close to a caress. "This time, stay loose. Let go and trust your instincts. If you don't, you'll get hurt."

Her gaze flashed to his as if to say, no matter what she did, she was bound to get hurt.

"To get from point A to point B and survive, a rider has to skim over obstacles," he told her. "Keep your eyes on the prize."

Sliding his hands down her arms, he started to pull her to her feet but she tugged her hands away and rose under her own steam, wincing as her skinned knee bent. She brushed away the dirt, leaving a smear of blood on her fingers.

"Just a little dirt rash," he said. "You'll get used to it."

She stared at him a moment then let out a burst of frustrated laughter. "You couldn't have taken up something civilized like tennis, could you? Oh, no, it had to be dirty and painful.''

She cycled away to take another run at the log. Eyes narrowed in concentration, she pushed off hard, getting up a good speed. Nate felt himself tense up as she approached, praying she wouldn't do another endo. This time when she bore down on the pedals and threw her weight back, the front wheel lifted. Triumph shone briefly in her smile before the wheel came down on the log and slid backward. She stuck out a leg to brace herself before she could fall.

Sean and Lee responded with derisive laughter which Nate cut off with a sharp look. ''We're all learning. We all make mistakes along the way.'' And to Angela, he said, ''That was a lot better. Next time throw your weight forward as soon as you're airborne.''

She took another run at the log and caught air, her front wheel rising just enough to clear the log. Her back wheel didn't make it to the opposite side. Shoulders slumped, she got off the bike and dragged it over.

''Take a rest and try again in a while,'' Nate suggested.

''I want to do it now. I think I know what I did wrong.''

''Okay, but how about trying that one.'' He

pointed to another log about twenty yards away, adding, "We should give the others a turn." And save her the embarrassment of repeatedly failing in front of the class.

She nodded and cycled off.

By the end of the lesson, all the kids had successfully bunny hopped over the log. Nate went in search of Angela and found her picking herself up off the ground. Her face was streaked with dirt and her knees were skinned and trembling with fatigue.

"Did you do it?" he asked.

Grim faced, she shook her head. "One more time."

"No." He gripped her by the wrist to prevent her from getting back on her bike. Then forgetting himself he pulled her into his arms and just held her. "You're too tired. Nothing will be gained by pushing yourself to the point of exhaustion."

He reached up and stroked the back of her head. Almost imperceptibly, she leaned into him and a rush of warmth flooded his heart. *Hell.* Lust he could conquer but where Angela was concerned tenderness would be his undoing.

"I tried so hard," she mumbled into his shirt.

"I know. Someday you'll do it. At the crucial moment, when you need to make that leap, you will soar."

"No, I won't," she sobbed, clinging to him as

if her legs were about to collapse beneath her. "Because I'll never walk or ride again."

Chuckling, Nate gently drew away. "Such a drama queen. You'll be a little stiff and sore tomorrow."

"A little!" She staggered to her bike. "I can't wait to go home and have a long soak."

Ricky rode up to them, still bouncing with energy, with Tim hot on his tail. "Can I go to Tim's for a barbecue and video?"

"My mom said it's okay," Tim told her.

"All right but Ricky needs to come home first to change and wash up," Angela replied.

"I'm not dirty," Ricky said with utter seriousness, gazing down at his filthy clothes and scraped knees.

Angela shook her head. "You're not getting away with that, bud. I may be soft but I'm not stupid."

"Aw, all right." Ricky turned his bicycle toward the easy trail that zigzagged down the mountain. "Hey, Tim, I'll race you."

Nate watched the boys tear off and said to Angela, "Since you're going to be on your own, why don't you come to my place for dinner and a soak in the hot tub? I guarantee it'll help ease those aching muscles."

Longing and indecision played over her face.

"Sounds wonderful but I'm not sure that's a good idea."

Probably it wasn't but he couldn't seem to help himself. "It's not a date," he said smoothly. "No law says we can't be friends."

"Since you put it that way... Thanks. I'll come by in about an hour?"

He wet his thumb with his tongue and wiped a smudge of dirt from the tip of her nose. "Perfect."

The door to Nate's house was standing open. Angela climbed the steep steps that would be buried in snow come winter, her gaze roaming over the two-story log home. The cedar-shake roof was steeply sloping in the alpine style to shed snow, and somehow she knew without being told that at the back of the house there would be a balcony overlooking the River of Golden Dreams. Living in a cramped apartment in the early days of their marriage she and Nate had talked about building a house together, sketching plans and dreaming their own golden dreams.

Reality check: *she'd* dreamed about a house; *he'd* fooled around on his mountain bike.

Then she'd left and he'd built the house without her. Typical.

"Hello," she called through the open doorway, peering into the deserted hallway. "Nate?"

This isn't a date, he'd said. Yet she'd tried on

three different outfits before settling on a sleeveless floral-patterned dress of pink and green on a white background. She'd put on new lipstick and her favorite perfume which also happened to be *his* favorite perfume. Wanting to feel pretty and feminine was only natural after a day spent grubbing around in the dirt. Wasn't it?

She found a doorbell set into one of the smooth rounded cedar logs and rang it.

No answer.

Drawn irresistibly, she entered the foyer. A contemporary hall table was topped by a large oval mirror and on the opposite wall hung a Haida painting in black, red and white. Her sandals were soundless on the carpeted hardwood floor as she went farther inside. It was like walking through the house she'd dreamed of. To the left was the living room, furnished in plump sofas of oxblood leather, cool to her fingertips. Around the L and into the dining room which looked as though it was never used for eating.

One end of the mahogany table was strewn with graph paper covered in histograms beside an open textbook showing wind patterns over the north Pacific Ocean. Wires ran from the ceiling, down the wall, to the back of a black console on the table. She peered to read the labels beneath the various dials: wind speed, barometric pressure, temperature....

The other end of the table held a computer. Some pages were stacked neatly to one side. She leafed through them and found they were descriptions of mountain-bike trails with accompanying hand-drawn maps. Was he writing a book?

Nate had developed more interests since she'd lived with him. And why not? Hadn't she grown and changed, too?

Her gaze roamed higher, to the collection of framed photos on the wall. There, among a cluster of Wilde family portraits, hung her and Nate's wedding photo. She looked impossibly young in her long satin dress and Nate unbelievably handsome in his father's black tuxedo. Cheek to cheek, they smiled into the camera, so certain their love would last forever. The irony was heartbreaking.

Where was the album of their photos that she'd left behind? All these years she'd had nothing by which to remember her brief marriage except a Polaroid snapshot of Nate on his bike that she'd had in her wallet when she ran away. That, and the images of him locked in her brain.

She continued through into the kitchen. Granite benchtops and gleaming stainless-steel appliances attested to the fact that he hadn't spared any expense here. She had to admit, his hard muscular body was an unbeatable advertisement for a regimen of exercise and healthy food.

Sliding-glass doors led to…ah, the balcony. These doors were open, too, and a light breeze carrying the scent of sun-warmed sap and wildflowers drew her outside. Towering white-capped mountains were etched against a crystalline blue sky and below flowed the glinting river. She breathed deeply, filling her gaze and her lungs with purity and beauty. In flat, traffic-clogged Toronto she'd longed for this vista, this mountain air.

Back in the hallway, she hesitated beside the stairwell. Upstairs almost surely held bedrooms while downstairs… A noise from below settled the question.

She went down to the semibasement, following the sound of low music from a radio. Coming to a door ajar, she pushed it open.

What in another house might have been a rumpus room was entirely given over to a workshop devoted to mountain bikes. Three bikes hung from hooks attached to the ceiling's cross beams. On the far wall, beneath a high window, level with the ground outside, a workbench held bicycle tools, spare inner tubes and old bike magazines. The red bike Nate usually rode stood in the center of the room clamped to a stand. It was surrounded by oily rags, bits of chain, tire levers, tins of lubricant and sundry wrenches.

Nate, his dark head bent forward, was crouched in front of the Balfa, whistling softly. Muscles moved in his tanned forearms as he adjusted the gears with adept fingers.

Angela cleared her throat and found it was unusually dry. ''Hi, Nate.''

CHAPTER SIX

"HELLO, GOLDILOCKS," Nate said, rising to his feet. "I see you've found your way to my den."

His swift allover glance bespoke compliments he probably didn't even realize he was sending her way. *Be still, heart.*

"Nice house," she said, coming closer. His freshly shaven jaw was shiny and the faint scent of lime aftershave cut through the smell of gear lubricant. Damp from the shower, his hair seemed darker than ever, and his neatly trimmed sideburns looked very masculine. "I recognize the design although it's easy to tell this is a bachelor pad."

"Don't knock it. There are plenty of advantages to bachelorhood."

"Such as?"

"No complaints about greasy bike parts inside the house."

"Can't argue with that." Angela picked her way past the debris on the floor to a glass case on the far wall which housed the many trophies he'd won over the years in both downhill racing and free-riding. How she used to hate those bike competitions and races he spent all his spare time training for—often when he should have been at work.

"Looks like you've won everything there is to win," she said. "How is your knee? You hurt it pretty badly in the downhill the year we got married."

"I had another operation last year. No big deal."

"No big deal. Right. Darn good thing you've stopped racing."

Nate bent over to gather up the tools on the floor and put them back into a pouch. "As a matter of fact, I've decided to ride in the Gravity Fest Air Downhill next month."

"But I thought you said—"

"It's the only major competition I haven't won and I'd really like to bag it before I retire. Besides, sponsorship proceeds will go to a children's charity."

Pursing her lips, she nodded, unable to fault the motivation behind his decision. But it just went to show he would never really give up competing, not completely.

Wandering farther, she came upon a child's bike hanging on the wall. The frame was dented and the black paint scratched; not exactly decorative. "What's this?"

"My first bike. My parents had it stored in their

garage—they never throw anything away. I came across it a couple of years ago and brought it over here.''

''Where you'll carry on the family tradition of never throwing anything away?'' she said, amused.

''I loved that bike. It was very special to me.'' He put down the screwdriver he'd been using and wiped his hands on a rag. ''You really like the house?''

''It's perfect. Just as we'd planned.'' Their gazes found each other's and she felt warmth rise to the surface of her cheeks. Turning away, she added, ''I mean, it should be good since you stole all my ideas.''

Nate tossed the rag aside and gestured to the door. ''Come upstairs. I'll open a bottle of wine. Unless,'' he added with a half smile, ''you want a quick lesson in stripping down a mountain bike.''

''*No, thanks.*'' She accompanied her vehement tone with a shudder. ''Do you know how long it took me to clean the dirt out of my nails after today's session?''

As she went past the workbench toward the door, a small silvery glint made her glance sideways. Hanging from a hook on the Peg-Board was the St. Christopher's medal she'd given him before his first big race of their marriage. It was shiny and untarnished. He'd kept it all these years and cared enough to polish it. She refused to think *that* was only another example of his pack-rat tendencies.

Upstairs, Nate opened a bottle of chilled white wine and they went through the sliding doors to the cushioned wooden chairs on the balcony. Angela twirled the stemmed glass between her fingers, admiring the golden glow of the fruity sauvignon blanc and feeling a little nervous. This might not be a date but it was starting to feel like one. Certainly it was the first occasion they'd deliberately arranged to get together for anything other than biking.

"Are these the wineglasses Janice gave us as a wedding present?" she asked.

"If you recall, I offered to give them back to you along with anything else your family and friends gave us," he said evenly. "You told me to keep everything because you wanted no tangible reminders of our marriage. If you've changed your mind and want the glasses, by all means, take them."

"I don't, and I'm sorry I mentioned them. You're quite right, I willingly relinquished all claim to our joint possessions. But..." She hesitated. "Do you still have our old photos? The ones I put into albums?"

"Ye-es. Do you want those?" He sounded more

reluctant to give up old photos than the Bavarian crystal.

"I just want to know they still exist."

"They're on the living-room bookshelf." He sipped his wine, regarding her thoughtfully. "Admit it, Ange. You should never have left."

She shifted uncomfortably in the soft cushions. "At the time, leaving seemed the only thing I *could* do. Separation was best for both of us."

"Do you really think you speak for me? What if I said I still loved you and wanted you back?"

She stared at him, unable to believe what she was hearing, afraid of the leap of hope that sprang to life inside her chest. "You couldn't love someone who ran out on you ten years ago," she said flatly, daring him to refute the point.

"Why not? What is true love if it isn't forever?"

"Do you really believe that?"

Nate got up to rest his elbows on the rail and look out at the river winding through the bushes. He glanced back at her, an odd smile on his face. "I'd have to be crazy to, wouldn't I?"

The shred of hope withered. "Why don't you admit you're still angry that I ran out on you?" she demanded. "Even now, as you stand there making light of our past, I bet you feel like strangling me."

Nate laughed. "If I wanted to strangle you I

would have done it years ago.'' Then he sobered. ''But I would never make light of our marriage. Or our breakup.'' He swirled the wine in his glass and added stiffly, ''Have you done anything about filing for divorce yet?''

''I can't until I go to Vancouver next.'' A cloud passed in front of the dying sun and the glow went out of the wine. ''Are we going to eat soon?'' she said. ''I'm starving.''

He set his glass down and moved past her to the far end of the balcony. ''I'll light the barbecue.''

They ate wild salmon and asparagus on the balcony while the setting sun turned the snowcapped peaks rosy. When Angela saw the white linen tablecloth set with their wedding dishes she very nearly burst into tears. Nate wasn't going to ask her to stay his wife. All she was losing—all she'd *thrown away*—suddenly was very dear to her. Oh, not the china or the silverware, but the peaceful times together, the laughter and quiet conversation.

She spoke little during dinner, except to murmur, ''This is delicious,'' after the first bite of charred flaky pink flesh melted on her tongue. The sun slipped behind the mountains as she ate the last lemony spear of asparagus. She shivered in her sleeveless dress and wrapped her arms around herself.

''Cold?'' Nate said. ''Let's get into the hot tub.''

She rose, wincing at protesting muscles that had already begun to stiffen, and helped Nate carry the dishes to the kitchen. "Leave them," he ordered when she would have stacked the dishwasher. "I'll get them later."

She grabbed her tote bag from the hall and followed him downstairs.

"Did you bring your bathing suit?" he asked.

"Of course. I'm not going skinny-dipping the way—"

The way they used to. In the dim light of the downstairs passage his gaze met hers. Every way she turned, it seemed, memories surfaced. Cool nights and hot flesh. Back then they hadn't had hot tubs at their disposal but the lake was free and glittering under the moonlight. She recalled the sensual swish of the water between her naked thighs, goose bumps rising as she ran dripping and laughing from the water with Nate in pursuit, to wrap together in a giant towel. Then lying on a blanket counting the stars before turning inward to gaze into each other's eyes...

"Where can I change?"

"In here." He opened a door to a spare bedroom with an en suite bathroom. "When you're ready, go out through that door." He pointed to an external door around the corner and down a short hallway. "You'll see the tub."

Angela strolled outside a few minutes later to find Nate already submerged up to his chest in frothing steaming water. Speakers attached to the outside wall under the wide eaves played Andean flute music and low fat candles glowed at intervals around the cedar platform supporting the hot tub.

Nate was good at setting the scene for romance when he wanted to; had she been naive about his motives in asking her here tonight? Or had she subconsciously wanted him to seduce her? She'd chosen her sexiest bathing suit, a blue one-piece cut high on the leg and showing plenty of cleavage. His appreciative gaze made her blood fizz with more than wine.

He smiled, his teeth gleaming white in the dusky twilight. "Come on in. The water's fine."

She lowered herself gingerly into the bubbling heated water, sinking up to her neck and sighing as the warmth penetrated her aching muscles straight through to her bones. Essential oils added to the water gave off scents of sandalwood and ylang-ylang. "That feels sooo good."

"And to think, all this could have been yours."

"Keep reminding me, why don't you?" She shut her eyes and leaned her head back on the fiberglass rim. "I'm doing just fine on my own, thank you very much."

"Where do you live in Vancouver?" he asked. "Have you bought a house, or an apartment?"

"I'm renting an apartment in the West End while I decide where to buy. I've got a good job at the magazine but, well, I just don't know. I could end up moving back to Toronto if things don't work out."

"You mean, getting hired permanently at the magazine?"

"Uh…yes."

"I'm surprised they let you work out of office, considering you'd only just started."

"Oh, that wasn't a problem. My predecessor, Penny, had set up a similar situation for herself since she had an hour and a half commute to work from Langley. She probably could have continued to work from home but she wanted to devote herself one hundred percent to her baby, at least in the beginning."

"What did you do in Toronto?"

"I was in the marketing department at the *Globe and Mail*. I left on good terms so I wouldn't have any trouble getting a job there again. If I wanted to, and a suitable position came up, that is." She opened an eye to see what he made of her potential future relocation but he wore what she used to think of as his Mr. Inscrutable face.

"Ever think of moving back to Whistler?"

Both her eyes opened. "Why would I want to do that?"

He just looked at her and she shifted on the seat, rotating her shoulders to ease the tightness.

"Come here," he said. "I'll give you a massage."

She hesitated, then slid across the hot tub, turning to sit in front of him with her back to him. The seat was broad, giving plenty of room for them both but the position was still intimate, especially when his fingers wrapped themselves around her shoulders and began to knead her aching flesh.

"You always did give the best massages," she murmured, shutting her eyes again and giving herself up to the pleasure of his touch.

He molded the stiff muscles in her neck and shoulders, then worked his hands down her arms which were sore from the strain of pulling up on the handlebars. The aromatic steam cleansed the dust from her sinuses, the flute music lulled her into a dreamlike state and within a short time her limbs began to feel like jelly.

It would be so easy to lean back and let Nate's muscular chest support her as he had so often in the past. Or to turn and weave her arms around his neck, lifting her face for his kiss. She'd dreamed of his kisses for years after she'd left, and still did, for that matter. Her lips parted slightly, thinking about his mouth on hers while his hands performed their magic on her arms.

His arms covered hers as his hands worked their way down her forearms, massaging the hurt out of deep places. His breath was warm on the back of her neck; she could hear it softly rasping with each rhythmic pulse of his fingers on her flesh. Gradually she sank into a semiconscious, sensual state, exquisitely receptive to touch, smell and sound. She'd never felt like this with anyone but Nate.

As if he were reading her thoughts and echoing them, he whispered, ''No one else turns me on the way you do, Angela.''

Now the water seemed to have heated to boiling point, turning her insides to liquid. She moved restlessly inside his arms, arching her back as the ache in her muscles faded and her focus moved to the heaviness in her breasts. She bit her lip, stifling a moan and opened her eyes a crack. The veins on his forearms stood rigid with tension. He was controlling himself, with difficulty, waiting for some signal from her.

''Nate...''

''Yes, Angela?'' His voice was guttural now, urgently questioning, implicitly agreeing to whatever she asked.

All at once she knew she couldn't go any farther.

"Let's not do anything we might regret," she said, pulling away with difficulty. She wanted him, yes, but not unless she had a solid reason to believe he still loved her. So far, nothing he'd said indicated he did.

"Regret?" Frustration choked his voice as his hands slid from her skin.

Then, through the fog of her overloaded senses, she heard a distant ringing. "What's that?"

His tension became a listening alertness. "The phone." Then he relaxed slightly. "The machine will pick it up."

She splashed water over her face, pushing back her hair. "What if it's Ricky?"

"I thought he was staying at Tim's until late."

"He is, but what if something's happened?"

He reached out, touched her cheek briefly. "You worry too much."

"Maybe. But please go answer the phone."

Nate rose dripping from the water, to wrap himself in the towel that was hanging on a deck chair. Without another word, he strode inside. She waited in the hot tub, telling herself she was being silly, that the phone call was for Nate and had nothing to do with Ricky.

Without Nate's presence her blood cooled, leaving her clearheaded and a little shocked at how far her defenses had lowered under his touch. In the hundred-degree water, she shivered. Her body ached still, but it wasn't from too much exercise. She'd been ready and more than willing for him to make love to her.

Thank goodness she'd called a halt to the proceedings. Surging upward out of the water, she reached for the other towel, water sluicing off her legs. Better she leave before her feelings got away from her again.

Footsteps sounded on the stairs and Nate appeared in the doorway. One glance at his pale face and her own turbulent emotions were forgotten. "What is it?"

"Ricky." Water dripped from Nate's hair and his fingertips. "He fell out of a tree. He's bleeding from the forehead. Kerry's pretty sure he's okay, but she called the ambulance, anyway. They're on the way to the emergency."

NATE DROVE TO THE EMERGENCY ROOM at Whistler Health Centre because Angela was too distraught. Thinking about what might have happened to Ricky scared him, too, but for her sake he held himself together. For perhaps the tenth time, he repeated, "Ricky's accident is not your fault."

"I should have been looking after him." She twined a strand of blond hair around her finger. "What am I going to tell Janice?"

"He didn't break any bones," Nate said calmly. "He got a gash on his forehead and he's shaken up. That's all."

"That's plenty! He's my responsibility and if I wasn't sitting in your hot tub—" She broke off and turned her face away but not before he caught her expression of shame and regret. And anger. At herself or him?

"What we were doing wasn't wrong." After a pause, he added, "You never used to mind when I touched you."

If he'd had his druthers, he'd have kissed her till they were both breathless, then taken her upstairs and made love to her all night long.

And then what? The question was sobering. He hadn't planned on seducing her but neither had he thought beyond the moment.

"You weren't *touching* me," she insisted. "You were massaging my sore muscles."

"Come on, Ange. You can't deny we were both turned on." He was tired of her endless denials. If only she would admit the big one, that she wanted him back in her life.

She dragged her fingers out of her hair and pressed them to her forehead. "Can we please not talk about this until I know that Ricky is all right?"

"Fine." She was close to tears, whether from worry over her nephew or angst about what happened in the hot tub, he couldn't tell. Either way, he didn't want to distress her further.

When they got to the hospital, Kerry was in the lobby, talking to the nurse on duty, while Tim roamed restlessly around the waiting room. Kerry saw them and left the nurses' station to greet them.

"Hi, Kerry," Nate said. "What's happening with Ricky?"

"He's getting stitched up. The nurse says he'll be fine." Kerry reached out and squeezed Angela's hand. "I'm so sorry."

"How did it happen?" Angela asked.

"The boys were playing in the backyard and their Frisbee landed in a tree. Ricky went after it. I happened to glance out the window and saw him twenty feet up, inching his way out onto a narrow limb. I tell you, I almost had a heart attack."

Tim came over, his attention caught by the discussion. "Ricky's been right to the top of that tree before," he declared. "He's not afraid of anything."

Nate put a friendly arm around Tim's shoulder. "Sometimes a little healthy fear will save your skin."

Angela asked Kerry, "Did he fall from that height?"

Kerry nodded. "I feel so responsible. I called

out and that distracted him. He lost his grip and slipped off the branch.''

Angela clutched her stomach. ''Oh my God.''

''The branch below broke his fall but he gashed his forehead on the way down.''

''I'll never forgive myself if anything else is wrong with him,'' Angela moaned. ''He might have killed himself, or been paralyzed.''

The matronly nurse, overhearing her, interjected, ''Don't fret. Ricky's going to be fine. He's a regular customer around here. I'm betting he'd be right back in that tree tomorrow given a chance.''

As she spoke, double swing doors banged opened and Ricky, his head bandaged, was pushed through in a wheelchair by a doctor in green scrubs. ''Who's in charge of this monkey?'' the doctor asked.

''I'm Ricky's aunt,'' Angela said, coming forward to crouch in front of the wheelchair. ''Honey, are you all right?''

'''Course, I'm all right,'' Ricky said cheerfully. ''This was nothing compared to the time I jumped off the garage roof.''

''I don't think I want to hear about that,'' Angela said faintly.

''No broken bones this time,'' the doctor told her, adding to Ricky, ''You're slipping, son.''

"Slipping," Angela repeated dryly. "That's very funny. How many stitches?"

The doctor threw her a commiserating glance. "Three, just above his right eyebrow. They'll dissolve in a week or so and he should heal up quickly." He clapped a hand on Ricky's shoulder. "Take it easy, young man. I don't want to see you in here again this summer."

Ricky's expression turned anxious as he glanced from Nate to the doctor. "This won't stop me from mountain biking, will it?"

"That's up to Angela," Nate replied. "But I don't see why not. What do you think, Doctor?"

"As long as the helmet doesn't chafe the bandage, Ricky should be okay to ride by the end of the week."

Ricky still didn't look happy. "That means I'll miss a lesson."

Nate gripped his shoulder. "Maybe not. The weather isn't looking too good for Tuesday. I might have to cancel the class."

"Good." Ricky seemed willing to take Nate's word for it. He turned to Angela. "Can I go back to Tim's house?"

"No, you may not," Angela said. "You're going straight home, where I can keep an eye on you."

Nate held out a hand to Ricky to help him out

of the wheelchair. "Come on, dude. I'll get you in the car."

"You can watch the movie another day," Kerry promised. As Nate walked ahead with Ricky, he heard her apologize again to Angela. "I'm really sorry. I feel terrible this happened at my house."

"It's all right," Angela assured her. "Don't worry."

"You're being very nice about it." After a pause, Kerry added politely, "Did Nate tell you about my brunch next Sunday? I hope you can make it."

"He did mention it, but...well, won't it be awkward?" Angela said hesitantly.

Nate was itching to turn around and see their faces but he kept walking, his ears tuned to the discussion going on between the two women.

"I don't see why," Kerry replied. She paused before adding, "I notice your hair is wet. When I couldn't get an answer at your house I called Nate but maybe you were home. I hope I didn't get you out of the shower."

"I was at Nate's. We were in the hot tub when you called." Angela sounded uncomfortable, as if she would have liked to deny even that.

"Ah," Kerry murmured knowingly.

"Don't get the wrong idea. Nate and I are just friends." Angela hastened to assure her.

"Really? I thought maybe you two were getting back together after all."

"No, I can't see that happening." Angela had lowered her voice but not so low Nate couldn't hear every word. "Too much water under the bridge." She paused. "I thought you two were going out."

"Not in the sense you probably mean. I think you're right," Kerry said. "Once it's over, it's over."

"Absolutely. Get on with life, that's what I say."

As the two women's voices became warmer and friendlier, Nate's blood pressure rose. For crying out loud! Could these women talk of nothing but how they *didn't* want an affair with him?

Nate opened the car door for Ricky then turned on them. "Will you two cut it out! Haven't you heard that the male ego is extremely fragile?"

They gazed at him with blank innocent faces then turned to each other and started to giggle. "So I'll see you next Sunday around eleven?" Kerry said to Angela.

"I'll look forward to it."

And then, before Nate's astonished eyes, the pair embraced as if they were bosom buddies.

Nate got into the car and waited for Angela to climb in on the passenger side. She immediately rolled down the window and waved to Kerry as they drove off.

The sky was almost dark now. Nate turned on the headlights as he pulled out of the hospital car park and onto the main road. "Is that how women talk to each other when they think a man isn't listening?"

In the dim light from the streetlights Angela gave him a pitying smile. "No, dummy, that's how women talk to each other when they know a man *is* listening."

He shook his head. "I don't get it."

"If you don't get it, then I can't explain it," she said airily. She gazed quietly out the window for a minute before turning back to him. "I don't understand. Kerry's really nice. And gorgeous. Why aren't you still dating her?"

"Why do you care?" He was a bit grumpy over the way they'd joined forces against him. And though he'd overused this tactic he tried it once more. "Jealous?"

"Ha!" She peered at him. "I do believe you're *trying* to make me jealous."

Interesting response; she hadn't denied it. "Why would I do that?"

"Because *you're* not over *me*."

One hand draped over the wheel, he threw her a lazy smile. "I already told you I still loved you."

She dismissed that with a flick of her polished nails. "Too glib. Too quick. You're always teasing."

"So, the brunch…" he said, moving on. "Shall we go together?"

"That would hardly be appropriate after I've told Kerry we're not involved, would it?"

"No, of course not," he muttered. "How are *you* doing, little dude?" he called to Ricky in the back seat. Men, he understood, even when they were only ten.

"Good," Ricky replied, cheerful and uncomplicated. "Auntie Angela, can I have some ice cream when we get home? I didn't get my dessert at Tim's."

"Sure, kiddo."

The time was on the hour so Nate turned on the radio and they listened to the news, followed by the weather. The forecast was for increasing cloud but no precipitation until late in the week when there was a chance of a thunderstorm.

"Darn," Ricky said from the back seat. "I guess you won't be canceling after all."

"My barometer readings suggest a change is coming sooner than that," Nate said. "We'll just wait and see."

A few minutes later, Nate pulled into Angela's driveway. He helped Ricky into the house and leaned against the kitchen counter while Angela got her nephew a big bowl of chocolate ice cream. Then he glanced at his watch. "I'd better get home and let you get Ricky to bed. He's had quite a day."

Angela walked him to the door. On the step, she crossed her arms and leaned against the doorjamb. "Thank you for dinner."

"Ricky's going to go nuts trying to stay quiet while he recuperates," Nate said. "What do you say we all go to a movie tomorrow night?"

"I can't," she said. "I still haven't finished my quarterly report, plus I need to teleconference with the editorial director. Circulation has slumped and one of our regular contributing writers moved to the States."

"Wednesday?"

"I really don't know if I'll have work sorted out."

"And Thursday I've got my meteorology class. I hope you'll be free on Friday for our first ride on a real trail."

Under the porch light he couldn't miss her involuntary flinch. "Will there be hills?"

"Look around you, Ange," he said, chuckling. "Do you see any spot on the horizon that *isn't* a hill? Don't worry, we'll go slowly."

"Oh, hey, I'm not worried." She paused, then added timidly, "What about logs?"

"No logs." Nate jingled his keys in his loosely closed fist. He didn't want to leave without resolving the constraint between them. "About what happened in the hot tub—"

"What *didn't* happen, you mean," she asserted.

"Still in denial," he said, shaking his head.

"*Good night,* Nate." She started to close the door, then paused and added in a milder tone, "Thanks for everything. I don't know what I would have done without your support tonight."

Nate had to summon all his self-control not to overstep unspoken boundaries and kiss her. "I would have done it for anyone."

"I know." She smiled. "That's why you're so terrific."

And so was she. "Good night, Ange. Sweet dreams."

CHAPTER SEVEN

FRIDAY MORNING, Angela strapped on her helmet and positioned the padding on her elbows, forearms, knees and shins. Butterflies were revving up in her stomach, ready for takeoff.

Nate had been right about the weather; Tuesday's class *was* canceled due to rain. On Thursday Ricky's doctor had given him the all clear to ride. Friday had dawned bright and sunny.

"Today's ride will be easy but fun," Nate told the class. Lee and Sean groaned theatrically, eager as always to hit tech trails.

Angela worried that Nate's idea of an easy ride and hers wouldn't coincide. He'd showed them the trail on the map and although it looked less difficult than some other trails, it had significant downhill sections.

Her thoughts were scattered and confused. She'd finished her report but hadn't been able to resolve the problems at the magazine over the telephone. And for days she'd been consumed with warring

doubts and desires regarding Nate, which undoubt-
edly contributed to her lack of focus at work.

He'd said twice now he loved her but how could
she believe him? Not only had he let her go, he'd
let her stay away for ten years. And even now, he
wasn't suggesting they try to reconcile; he was taking it for granted that she'd admit she never wanted
a divorce in the first place. She got shivers thinking
how close he was to being right. His protestations
of love were facile and yet, the way he looked at
her kept her coming back for more.

"However, you *will* encounter obstacles along
the way," Nate was saying. "To get the cleanest
ride, you need to develop your off-road vision."

"What's that?" Lisa wanted to know.

"It's a way of looking at the trail. Don't stare
at what you want to miss, like a big rock or a tree
root. Your bike follows your eyes. Instead, scan
ahead for obstacles and then trust your computer—" he rapped his knuckles against his head
"—to plot a clear course. Think of it like a chess
game—you're planning several moves ahead with
your eyes on the ultimate prize."

His eyes came to rest on Angela. "Ready?"

"Of course," she said, tossing him a carefree
smile. Silently she repeated her mantra, *I will not
wimp out, I will not wimp out....*

They set off from the parking lot of the Whistler

Interpretive Forest south of the resort, rattling across the wooden bridge over the Cheakamus River then climbing the gentle slope of the wide smooth Riverside Trail for several miles. When they came to another dirt parking lot Nate guided them through a gated road up a hill that had Angela dropping into granny gear before she'd gone ten yards.

"Use your arms," Nate said, circling back to ride beside her. "Pull yourself up the hill."

"What...do...you...mean?" She sounded like an asthmatic, the way she gasped for oxygen between each word. Glancing sideways at Nate, who wasn't even breathing hard, she saw that with every downward stroke of his pedal the muscles of his forearms stood out as he exerted a backward force on his handlebars. It made no sense to her but she tried it and found the extra torque helped.

I will not wimp out. I will not wimp out.

She watched him ride ahead. Since the night in the hot tub and the reawakened awareness of each other's bodies, their relationship had altered subtly. Although Nate had said or done nothing suggestive, all day she'd felt his gaze on her, felt his *mind* on her. This morning she'd realized with a jolt that while she'd been plodding along, reacting to each encounter with him as though it were an isolated incident, he'd been taking note of obstacles and mentally skipping ahead to his goal—making love with her. Oh, he hadn't come out and said that's what his aim was but she knew him well enough to know what was on his mind. Whether *he* knew it or not.

At last she crested the hill and followed the group down an offshoot of the main trail that crossed a creek. Sean and Lee had splashed through in water up to their axles and Nate was giving them a lecture on the perils of ruining their bikes by getting them wet and then adding dust and dirt to the mix.

"There will be times when you won't be able, or want to keep dry," he added. "But there's no glory in getting your chains and gears so mucked up they rust out when you need them most."

Angela got off her bike and hoisted it over her shoulder, picking her way across the water. If she was good at anything, it was keeping clean. Nate nodded his approval as she set the dry bike down on the other side.

Up and down, and up again, back to the logging road. Angela's calves started to burn and her throat was dry. Finally a single track beckoned them into the woods and soon they were riding through an ancient stand of cedars. Just when she thought her legs would give out completely, Nate gave the signal to stop for lunch.

Dismounting, Angela staggered over to a huge log covered in thick moss. She removed her helmet and her shoes and socks, and lay flat on her back on the cool cushioned surface. She barely had the energy to lift her drink bottle to her mouth but somehow she managed, even with her eyes closed. Then she squirted water over her face, cooling her burning cheeks.

"You're doing great, Ange." Nate's hand gripped her shoulder briefly and his voice was warm with approval.

Opening her eyes, she saw his broad shoulders black against the sun and felt a flutter in her stomach. Had she fooled him the other night into thinking she wasn't moved by his touch? Or was she only fooling herself?

Before she could speak, he moved on, pausing for a casual word with each of the kids that left them quietly beaming. The others had recovered quickly and were devouring their packed lunches in gulps, like ravenous dogs. Angela dragged herself upright and got her brown bag out of the saddle pack.

"Mind if I join you?" Nate was back, with his own lunch. He'd removed his helmet and his thick black hair was damp and flattened at the temples.

"Be my guest." She gestured to the expanse of

mossy log, hoping he would take the hint and leave some distance between them.

He sat right next to her, close enough that she could feel the heat radiate from his bike shirt. A sheen of perspiration coated his tanned arms, highlighting the sculpted muscle. "Tired?" he asked.

"No."

"Liar."

He grinned at her, and she couldn't help but smile. She was tempted to push him off the log, maybe wrestle him to the ground. Briefly she fantasized about them making love on the cool mossy floor of the forest.

Instead she ate her slightly squishy sandwich while the flutter in her stomach intensified.

"Nate, can we go exploring?" Ricky called.

"Go ahead but don't wander too far. And don't fall off anything." As the children scrambled into the woods he turned back to Angela. "Want to take a walk?"

"Is that a stream I hear? I wouldn't mind dipping my feet in cool water."

"Come with me." He slid off the far side of the log and picked a way through hummocks of decaying logs in the fern-covered forest. The air was moist and rich with the scents of humus and cedar. The shouts and laughter of the children became . muted by the giant trees as the sound of running water grew louder. Filtered sunlight lit patches of tea-colored stream that tinkled over smooth stones and past glistening roots jutting from the bank.

Angela sat on a rock and hung her bare feet in running water so cold it stung. She drew her breath in sharply, biting her lip to force herself to keep her feet submerged.

Nate dropped down beside her. "Don't you miss this, living in the city?"

Leaning back, she stared up at the giant trees tapering to distant points against the blue sky. She closed her eyes and dug her fingers deep into the springy moss, breathing in the earthy scents of the man beside her. "All the time."

A tickling, featherlike touch against the base of her throat made her put up a hand to brush it away. Her fingers encountered a fern frond. She opened her eyes and met Nate's intent dark gaze.

Now that he had her attention, Nate tossed away the frond. "Remember our picnic spot on top of Whistler?"

The scene of their first kiss on a secluded knoll high on the mountain. She nodded, knowing he was about to kiss her again. As his mouth drew slowly nearer she realized they'd been approaching this kiss ever since they'd run into each other in the supermarket.

His lips, warm and firm, touched hers with a

sweetness that made her want to cry. He tasted of the forest and fresh air and the solid strength of the mountain. The suppressed yearning in her heart bubbled to the surface and she eased her arms around his neck. He broke the kiss to look at her and the heat in his eyes was enough to melt granite. Then his mouth found hers again and her fingertips brushed his faintly raspy jaw.

Their intimacy was strange and familiar all at once: exciting like embarking on a journey, safe like coming home. The years fell away and all she knew was the need to rebond. When he drew back again she moaned in protest.

"Do you want me as much as I want you?" he whispered against her temple.

"Yes," she breathed.

"Say it."

"I want you."

Groaning deep in his throat, his arms crushed her to him while he pressed kisses over her closed eyes, her nose, her cheeks. "You should never have left me."

"I made a mistake." Her mouth sought his blindly and he tantalized her with a brief kiss.

"You love me," he crooned.

"I— Hey, what is this?" Something was wrong here.

"What is what?" He tried to kiss her neck.

"You, feeding me lines." She struggled out of his arms, uneasiness washing over her like cold water. "Why?"

Nate sat upright, frowning. "I don't know what you're talking about. We were kissing and making up."

"We were not. You were telling me what I should be feeling. And saying. You're trying to manipulate me." She scrambled to her feet, only to hop around on the stream bank with icy pins and needles in her feet.

"I was not."

"You were, too. You deliberately seduced me so you could get me to say whatever you wanted. Next you'll be saying our breakup was my fault."

"Well, it was!"

"God damn it, Nate. Can't you accept responsibility?"

"Can't *you?* If you'd told me how unhappy you were, I might have been able to change. If you hadn't run away we might have talked and worked things out."

"You let—"

"Don't say it," he warned. "It's a cop-out."

"I— You—" she sputtered, then went silent, staring at him. He was right, damn him. "Okay! I *am* partially responsible. I shouldn't have left without trying to work through our problems. Are you happy?''

All these years she'd been building him up in her mind as the villain and herself the wronged one. But that was false. As false as his kisses. She couldn't bear it that he was using her feelings for him against her.

She picked up her socks and shoes and strode off back to the log where she'd left her bike. The clearing was empty; the kids must still be playing in the woods.

''Where are you going?'' Nate demanded, following.

She jammed her wet feet into her shoes and socks and plunked her helmet on her head. ''You don't actually care about me. You just wanted to get me to admit I was wrong because your pride won't allow you to take the blame. Well, I've admitted my part in our marriage breakup. Fair enough. Now I'm leaving.''

Nate crossed his arms over his chest, his expression dark and glowering. ''You can't leave without me.''

Angela grabbed her bike and threw her leg over. ''Watch me.''

Adrenaline fueled by anger lent Angela strength and she pumped the pedals hard, backtracking to the main trail. Nate shouted for her to come back. She ignored him.

Let him yell and carry on, she thought, veering left at the junction. She was in charge of her own destiny, right down to finding her way back home without his help.

She glanced over her shoulder. He wasn't following. A lump formed in her throat. That was just so typical.

The trail dipped, and her gaze snapped forward. This wasn't the way they'd come! The single-track trail before her ran steeply downhill, looping around trees and boulders before disappearing around the slope of the mountain.

Panicking, she squeezed hard on the levers of both brakes. The bike's forward progress halted with a sudden jolt that almost threw her over the handlebars. Just in time she eased off the brakes, hearing Nate's voice in her head saying, *Feather your front brakes on a steep downhill.* Which was the front brake? Her right hand squeezed tentatively. That was it!

Her moment of elation quickly vanished in the face of a more immediate danger. The hard-packed dirt trail was suddenly a dense rubble-strewn path. She jolted over the embedded rocks, every vibration shooting painfully up her spine and her stiffened arms. Her top teeth banged into her bottom teeth and her eyes felt as if they would bounce right out of their sockets.

This was insane. She'd never make it down the hill alive. She had to stop and turn around, even if it meant pushing her bike all the way back up. She was reaching for her brakes when she remembered something else Nate had said. *Keep loose.*

A light went off in her head. That would be the "ready" position he was always hammering into them—butt off the seat, elbows and knees relaxed to absorb the shock. She raised her bottom above the saddle and made a conscious effort to bend her elbows. Miraculously, the jolting was reduced immediately. She rounded the slope of the mountain. She could almost enjoy this—

If it weren't for that Douglas fir up ahead, smack in the middle of the trail. Which way around, the high side or the low? The high side was narrower but the low... She shuddered at the prospect of sliding away on the scree of eroded hillside below the fir tree. The fir was coming at her too fast for her to make a decision.

Trust your instincts, Nate's voice bellowed in her mind. *Let go.*

At the last second she planted her seat on the saddle and swerved to the high side. She lifted her knees to her chin and held her breath, praying she wouldn't leave half her leg scraped off on the tree.

The pedal hit the tree, the bike wobbled dangerously. Angela extended a leg for balance and, by some miracle, managed to remain upright. A grin spread across her face. Her form was probably lousy and she hadn't followed the rules—whatever they were—but she'd made it intact around the tree and was still cycling.

Now she had a goal—to get to the bottom with a clean run. She could, and she would.

The single track entered the forest again, running straight and smooth through a grove of fir and hemlock. Like a pro, she banked around bends, raised herself off the saddle to bump loosely over hillocks, touched the front brakes to slow her pace as she traversed a washout. She hardly touched the brakes now, going faster and faster, confident and aggressive as she wove among the trees. Over an undercut bank she flew—she'd caught air!

Flying and styling. Mind-body fusion. What a buzz!

In a gap through the trees, she glimpsed the river with the railway tracks running parallel. She was almost to the bottom! Just around the next bend...

A log lay across the path. It disappeared into the undergrowth on either side of the trail, leaving her no way around it short of bush bashing. Doubt thrilled down her spine, leaving her skin clammy with cold sweat. Her fingers flexed toward the brake lever. If she didn't stop she would crash and burn.

Soar over obstacles.

She rose off the saddle and pushed hard on the pedals, increasing her speed, riding straight at the log.

At precisely the correct moment, she pressed down on the handlebars, compressing the wheel, then lifted, shifting her weight back off the front tire. The wheel rose in the air. Was it high enough? Would she make it? With all her might and determination she threw herself forward, willing the bike to clear the log. The front wheel was over. The back wheel bumped and dragged on the log, then it, too, was over. Relief poured through her, followed by an exhilaration exceeding anything she'd ever known.

Seconds later she coasted into the clearing where the trail had left the gravel road. Grinning foolishly, she circled the empty parking lot to imaginary applause and cheers.

Until Nate tore out of the woods into the clearing. "What the hell did you think you were doing!"

"Nate!" she cried, taking no notice of his angry shout. "I did it! I cleaned the trail." She circled around him, still ablaze, unable to understand why he didn't share her excitement.

"Never, *ever* take off like that," he raged. "You could have broken your bloody neck!"

"I know! The trail was a minefield of obstacles." She couldn't stop chattering, her enthusiasm tumbling out of her in quick broken sentences. "The tree. And those rocks. I bunny hopped. Nate, can you believe it?" With a whoop, she popped a wheelie.

When she landed Nate grabbed her handlebar and held her still. "I had to leave the rest of the class to come after you. Some of them might not have your luck negotiating that hill on their own."

His harsh words and furious gaze finally penetrated. "Oh my God. I didn't think. Ricky—"

"No, you *didn't* think. That's the trouble with you. You just take off, with no regard for others."

"I'm sorry, Nate. I know it was dumb—"

"It was worse than dumb, it was dangerous. For yourself and for the others. I've a good mind to cut you from the class."

"You can't do that," she said, alarmed that he might actually carry through his threat.

"I can and I might. Right now I can't waste time talking. The rest have started down and I've got to make sure they're all right." As he started to pedal away he gave her one final scowl. "Don't go anywhere."

Sobered, Angela rode to the edge of the clearing,

got off her bike and sat at a picnic table. The wait
was agonizing, her imagination conjuring all the
potential disasters she hadn't had time to think of
as she'd careened down the track. Then she heard
voices and her head lifted. Sean came shooting out
of the woods, closely followed by Lee. Then one
by one came the others. Except Ricky.

Angela started to jog toward the trail. Ricky bar-
reled into the clearing, both hands raised in the air,
whooping and hollering. Pretty much as she must
have looked, she thought wryly. Fine for a kid, but
she was glad no one had been waiting there to see
her.

They were all talking at once, laughing and
comparing notes about the trail. Sean had grazed
his leg on the tree and was proudly showing off
his bloody skin. Lisa had fallen going over the
rocks, but so slowly she hadn't hurt herself. David
and Mark had chickened out and carried their bikes
over the fallen log. Jill, Lee, Ricky and Tim had
cleaned the trail and were stoked.

"We weren't supposed to take this loop," Nate
began, and the group hushed. "There were some
technical points I wouldn't have thrown at you the
first time out—"

"Hurray, Angela, for making us follow the
wrong path," Ricky shouted.

Angela wanted to sink into the gravel.

"When are we riding the Khyber Pass?" Sean shouted.

"When you're a much more advanced rider than you are today." Nate's severe tone dampened even Sean's rebellious exuberance. "The Khyber Pass is one of the most difficult single tracks around Whistler. The trail you just came down is moderately easy."

This pronouncement brought a shocked silence to the group, Angela included. That was *easy?* She'd hate to see difficult.

"You all handled it well, even those who fell or dismounted," Nate added more kindly, his gaze resting briefly on David and Mark. "A wise man knows his limits. That log will still be there the next time you ride this trail."

He glanced at the sky and the clouds that had started to mass against the mountain. "We'd better head back before it rains."

In single file, the children set off, retracing their path down the gravel road on the route to Whistler. Nate rode down the line, his gaze automatically scanning each bicycle he passed for evidence of problems before they hit the highway. When he reached Angela, his face became set and hard.

"I'm really sorry about taking off," she began, hoping to forestall another lecture.

"Taking off is what you do," he said, circling

her. "What you don't do is think through the consequences of your actions. That's hardly a good example to set for Ricky."

"I was wrong, I admit it. And I've apologized. Lighten up," she said, losing her patience. "There was no harm done in the end."

He wouldn't look at her. Didn't speak.

"You're overreacting," she went on, getting more annoyed. "Your anger is out of proportion to the incident."

"Is it?" His dark burning gaze turned on her. "Or is it exactly in proportion to your behavior?"

It didn't take an Einstein to know he wasn't talking about an illicit ride down the bike trail.

CHAPTER EIGHT

NATE MADE HIMSELF salad and steak and tried to work on his compendium of bike trails but he couldn't concentrate. He thought he would have cooled down by now but his ire continued to bubble up from some deeper source than he'd been aware of till now. To make matters more confusing he felt badly about chewing Angela out. She'd been partially right about his motives for kissing her and he didn't like what that said about him. Nor was he comfortable with the emotions the kiss had revived.

Switching off the computer he went downstairs to take his bike for a ride. He guessed it wasn't surprising when he found himself on the road to Janice and Bob's house.

Angela answered the door. Regarding him with a wariness just short of inhospitable she stood back to let him enter. "Come to the kitchen. We're finishing dinner."

Chinese takeout, by the looks of the cartons scattered over the table. Ricky's plate was empty and he was trying to pick up a grain of rice with chopsticks.

"Can I get you something?" she asked coolly. "Cup of cold coffee? Congealed noodles?"

"No, thanks." He turnèd to Ricky. "How's your forehead? Did the stitches survive today's ride?"

"Yup. The helmet didn't even rub on the bandage." Ricky gave up on the grain of rice and cracked open a fortune cookie. "Listen to this— 'Life's journey has its ups and downs.' It sure did today!"

Despite himself Nate chuckled and happened to catch Angela's eye. She smiled reluctantly and for a brief moment they shared enjoyment of Ricky's enthusiasm. Would they have stayed together if they'd had children? The thought brought a lump to his throat and he cleared his windpipe to dislodge it.

To Angela, he said, "Can we talk?"

She glanced at the wall clock. "Ricky, that TV show you wanted to watch started two minutes ago."

With a yelp, Ricky pushed back his chair and ran into the living room. A few seconds later, the familiar theme song of a popular kids' show sounded from the TV.

Angela sat opposite Nate. "So, where do we start?"

"How about with you running away." Their problems went back further than that but her leaving tied in with the trigger that had sparked today's episode.

"We've done that. How about with why you didn't come looking for me after that bike race?"

"Janice told me you'd gotten on a bus and went back East. I was angry and...humiliated." Just thinking about how humiliated made him angry all over again. "I deliberately put you out of my mind. My family kept telling me not to worry, that you'd be home when you were ready."

"And you accepted that," she said flatly.

"Not entirely. After your letter, which made no sense at all, by the way, I bought a plane ticket to Toronto. I never got a chance to use it. Two days before my flight I had the accident that resulted in the first knee operation."

"I didn't know," she said quietly.

"Because you didn't listen to anything Janice said about me, did you?" He was guessing here.

"I meant, I didn't know you bought a plane ticket—how could I? I heard about the operation."

Nate fell into a resentful silence. She'd known about his accident and hadn't even called to find out how he was.

As if she knew what he was thinking, she said, "I was still angry about your obsession with biking. I told myself it served you right. I did ask Janice for regular updates on your recovery."

"Maybe if you understood why I love biking so much—"

"I know, I know, you're a Jedi master."

"No," he said impatiently. "You know that old black bike of mine, the first one I ever had?"

"Yes." Her eyes glazed over slightly and she began to pick up scattered sesame seeds with the pad of her finger.

"My parents gave it to me when I was recovering from Perthes as a child. Learning to ride had a profound effect on me."

Angela stopped gathering seeds and frowned. "I beg your pardon? Perthes—what is that?"

He hated talking about it, hated the memories it invoked and the weakness it implied. But she needed to know this about him. "Legg-Calvé-Perthes disease. It's a disease which affects young children, mostly boys. It causes the tip of the femur where it sits in the hip socket joint to disintegrate. My leg had to be immobilized in a splint, but apparently I kept pushing the limits so the doctor had me confined to bed with my leg strapped down for six months."

Angela looked as though she'd just been told the

sky was green instead of blue. "Six months! I can't imagine someone as active as you being immobilized for even a short period of time let alone half a year."

Nate shrugged. "You think I'm active now, you should have seen me as an eight-year-old. I just about drove my mother crazy except that she felt so sorry for me."

"It must have been horribly traumatic for you," Angela said with feeling.

"I was lucky—I was diagnosed early and made a full recovery. The bike was to help strengthen my legs. The first time I wobbled down the driveway I felt as though I'd been given wings." He smiled, remembering. "From that day on, Mom and Dad couldn't get me *off* the bike."

"Why didn't you ever tell me about this before?"

He shrugged and glanced away. "Being a bedridden invalid, even as a child, doesn't exactly fit with my macho image." He paused and looked back at her. "Would knowing have made a difference back then?"

"I don't know," she admitted. "Probably I'd still have wished I'd been your *only* passion. I was—" she grimaced "—a little immature. But that was part of our problem. We both were." She grinned suddenly. "Macho man, eh?"

Nate rolled his eyes, acknowledging her point.

"What about after you recovered from the knee operation?" Angela went on, returning to the subject. "Why didn't you come after me then?"

"I was offered sponsorship by a big mountain-bike manufacturer." He saw the flash of hurt on her face, quickly masked. "That was a very big deal for me, Ange. At last, I was going to make serious money from my sport. Plus, knowing how you felt about financial security I figured that with cash in my pockets you'd be more inclined to come back.

"If you'd wanted to, that is. By that time I was convinced you'd realized you'd never loved me and were using the fight as an excuse to stay away." He paused but she neither denied or confirmed his hypothesis. "Anyway, for a couple of years I hit the trails hard—entering competitions, trialing bikes, helping the company with research and development. When I had enough money for a deposit, I bought the bike store."

"So you had lucrative work, a stable lifestyle and a promising future. Yet you still didn't come and find me." She fiddled with her chopstick. "I guess by then you'd fallen out of love with me and were going out with other women—"

"Hang on. Our separation wasn't all one-sided," he said forcefully. "You were living with another guy! Janice was forever telling me how well you were doing, going to college, getting a job in publishing. You'd moved on, left me behind.'' He picked up a fortune cookie, turning it over in his hands. ''Besides,'' he added reluctantly, ''the longer I left it, the harder it became to call you. You should have been the one to come home since it was you who left me.''

She didn't speak but the message was in her eyes, clear as the air they breathed. *You let me go.*

Nate broke open the fortune cookie and the dry slip of paper rustled in his fingers as he unfurled it. What he read made his lips curl in a sardonic smile. '' 'Happiness awaits you.' Good thing I'm a patient man.'' He pulled another cookie from the plastic bag and sent it skittering across the table to Angela. ''Go on.''

''I don't believe in that stuff.''

''You don't have to. It's supposed to be fun.''

As if humoring him, she broke open the cookie and silently read her fortune. Without a word she crushed the paper in her palm and tossed it into an empty takeout box, blinking hard. ''This is just stupid.''

Nate eyed the box, wondering how something stupid could upset her almost to the point of tears. He slid a flattened hand across the table till his fingertips just touched hers. "I'm sorry for yelling at you today."

Her shoulders stiff, she pulled her hand away and dug the heel of it into her eyes, wiping away moisture. *"Why?"* she demanded, angry and beseeching. "Why do you charm me into your arms one minute and shout at me the next?"

"I wanted you to admit you made a mistake in leaving."

"And I did. You banter and tease but deep down you are still angry at me. I don't want to be on tenterhooks, never knowing when I'll end up on the receiving end again. Your apology is meaningless unless you back it up with an explanation."

"I—" He broke off, clenching his fists among the scattered chopsticks and used napkins. He hadn't wanted to spill his guts but it looked as though he had no choice. "I *loved* you. I wanted us to be a family. With kids." He sucked in a deep breath. He had to get this out quickly. "You didn't value that as much as you wanted material things—money, a career, success. You didn't believe I would provide for you—for us. Do you have any idea how that feels to a man?"

She stared in silence, her eyes huge in a pale face.

"It made me feel like—" He broke off again; he'd never been good at describing his feelings, especially when they made him appear weak. "—like a failure. As though even if I'd won every competition in the world I'd still be no good in your eyes. As though the very thing that makes me who I am is the thing that makes you not want me. As though you're saying to me, don't be who you are, because I can't love that person." He let out a long sigh. "And I guess that turned out to be true."

He waited for her to deny it. Her face was a frozen mask, her white-knuckled fingers clenched around a chopstick, pressing on it just short of breaking point.

"Can you blame me for wanting to escape my mother's fate?" she said in a low taut voice. "I wanted babies, too, but not so soon. We barely had enough to feed, clothe and shelter ourselves. Whistler is an expensive place to live and we were just getting by. Besides, I wanted to make something of myself, go to college."

Nate stared at her, for the first time truly seeing their situation from her point of view. He'd been selfish, thinking only of his own dreams, taking it for granted they were enough for both of them.

"You could have had children first, then got your education," he suggested, reluctant to give up a decade-long belief in the rightness of his actions. "Or done them both at the same time."

''What if we couldn't find the money?'' she re-
torted. ''Or our marriage broke down? We were so
young—it happens all the time.''

''Again, you showed no faith,'' he protested, but
feebly.

''Yeah, but *I'd* be the one who was stuck. I had
no intention of eking out an existence in some flea-
bitten one-room apartment with a squalling baby,
thank you very much.''

''No matter what, I wouldn't have left you to
cope alone.'' Her hard skeptical gaze showed she
didn't believe him. ''Even so…'' he added slowly,
''I shouldn't have pressured you to have children
when you weren't ready.'' He let out a deep sigh.
''You got what you wanted on your own, a career
and financial success.''

If possible, she turned even paler. ''It came at a
terrible cost.''

''You mean, our marriage?''

She shrugged as if pulling on a mantle of indifference. ''We barely knew each other, didn't have
the communication skills to work through our
problems and had no compelling reason to stay together when the going got rough.''

Except love, Nate thought. He was about to say
that in spite of the heartache he'd cherished their
time together when old resentments surfaced. This
was so like Angela, forcing *him* to profess his de-

votion yet giving nothing away of her own emotions. "Maybe you're right. Our marriage was a mistake on every level."

Ricky ran into the kitchen, sliding on the polished linoleum. "Can I get myself some ice cream?"

"All right." Angela gazed down at her folded hands, silently avoiding Nate's eyes while Ricky, cheerfully unaware of the tension between them, got the ice cream out of the freezer. Or *was* he unaware, Nate wondered, catching Ricky's sidelong glance at his aunt. But if he knew they were fighting, he didn't let on as he scooped mounds of chocolate ripple into his bowl.

Nate rose. Expressing his anger had helped to dissipate it but left him drained. "I'd better go. We can talk tomorrow."

Angela lifted her head. "I have to go to Vancouver tomorrow. The editorial director called a meeting to tackle some of the problems we're having at the magazine. Also—"

He waited silently for her to finish. *She had to file for divorce.* He wasn't going to help her out.

"—I'll have to take Ricky and stay overnight, possibly for a couple of days."

Ricky put the ice-cream container back in the freezer and sat at the table. His anxious gaze moved from Angela to Nate. "We won't miss a bike class, will we?"

"I'm afraid so, Ricky." Angela rubbed at her forehead but she couldn't erase the lines between her eyebrows.

"Ricky can stay with me until you get back," Nate found himself saying, feeling sorry for the boy. "I can give him some odd jobs at the store."

"Cool!" Ricky said.

"I couldn't possibly impose on you," Angela protested stiffly.

"He wouldn't be any trouble," Nate said. "He'd enjoy the bike shop more than the office of a woman's magazine."

"I sure would," Ricky agreed. "Please, Angela."

"I don't know what Janice would say," Angela said slowly. "Ricky's my responsibility."

"Call her and ask," Ricky pleaded.

"Can you?" Nate said.

"She gave me their itinerary with the phone numbers of all the hotels they're staying at. I could call—if you're sure he wouldn't be in your way," Angela finished doubtfully.

"He'll be fine." He found a smile for Ricky. "You can help me with my weather instruments. We'll try to figure out when the next big storm will be."

"Oh boy!" Ricky exclaimed. Then he heard the main cartoon character loudly bemoaning his tragicomic fate and raced back to the living room.

"If Janice agrees," Nate added to Angela, "you can drop him off at the store. I'll be there all day tomorrow."

"Thank you, that would be a huge help." Angela held herself carefully, as if she were so brittle she might break. "I'll call Janice once I work out the time difference between here and Europe. Now, if you'll excuse me, I need to go pack." Before he could say goodbye, she, too, hurried from the room.

"I'll just let myself out," Nate said to the empty kitchen.

He turned to go, then paused and shook the takeout box upside down. Picking up the slip of paper, he straightened it out and read Angela's fortune.

You will be lucky in love.

NATE SAT DOWN WITH RICKY the next evening after work and went over his weather data with the boy. "There are two columns for each weather indicator. One for observed measurements collected from the electronic weather station I installed on my roof, and the second for my predicted temperature, barometric pressure, wind speed, et cetera."

"Can I go up on the roof and see your weather station?" Ricky asked eagerly.

"No," Nate said bluntly. "But you can read the figures off the digital display unit on this console."

"Can we send up a weather balloon?"

"We don't have the budget for that, I'm afraid."

Ricky, head in hand, leaned on the table and frowned at the rows of columns. "What's this third one?"

"That's information supplied to me from the meteorology department. I compare my predictions to theirs. Most days I give them a pretty good run for their money.

"Back to the console," Nate continued. "I take two readings a day, at six in the morning and six at night." Nate glanced at the clock. "It's just 6 p.m. now. Write this down…temperature, 21 degrees Celsius—barometric pressure, 1015 millibars…."

They worked together for the next few minutes, Nate reading the numbers off the dials and Ricky recording the data in the columns. When they were finished, Nate said, "Tomorrow morning, you can read the dials while I record. Do you think you can wake up at six o'clock?"

"I've got an alarm on my watch," Ricky said, holding up his wrist so Nate could see his digital watch. "I'll set it now so I don't forget. See, it's this button here."

"Pretty cool," Nate said.

"Angela gave it to me last Christmas—she always gives the best presents."

Angela. She'd barely said two words to him when she'd dropped Ricky off at the store that morning; she'd been in a hurry and he'd been busy with a customer. But those few words were devastating.

"Are you going to file?" he'd asked tersely as she'd headed for the exit.

She'd stared at him. "The documents are in my briefcase."

He should have expected as much yet the way his heart sank had come as a shock.

There was a knock at the open door and Aidan's voice called out, "Anyone home?"

"We're in the weather-science center," Nate replied, winking at Ricky.

Aidan appeared in the doorway with Emily, in a pink dress and a halo of yellow curls, close behind.

"Did you come over to find out what the weather will be tomorrow?" Ricky asked.

"No, I came to complain about the rain we had today." Aidan brushed droplets from his hair with a quick sweep of his hand. "It wasn't forecast."

"You relied on the newspaper report, didn't you?" Nate tsked gently. "Next time check with me."

"I'll do that. I see you've got an assistant," Aidan added, smiling at Ricky.

"You remember Angela's nephew, Ricky. He came with her to Mom's birthday."

"Hi, Ricky. This is Emily."

"Hi," Ricky replied and Emily ducked behind her father's leg.

Nate turned to Ricky. "I'm going to visit with Aidan now. Do you want to plot the data we collected today on this set of graphs?"

Ricky nodded, so Nate showed him how to graph the data then left him to it, with Emily watching the dials on the weather console. As he and Aidan went out he heard Ricky inform Emily, "The barometric pressure is twenty-five millibars higher today than yesterday. That means the weather's changing and it's going to get sunny."

Nate exchanged a smile with Aidan. "How's things on the mountain?"

Aidan perched on a bar stool while Nate made coffee. "We found the two lost hikers. They were suffering from mild hypothermia but otherwise okay."

"I'm glad to hear it." Nate handed him a steaming mug and they went out onto the balcony. The rain had slowed to intermittent showers, dripping off the roof onto the log railing.

"What's up with you?" Aidan asked. "How are things with Angela?"

Nate filled Aidan in on the events of the past week culminating in the previous night's hashing out of the incidents surrounding her leaving. "She's gone to Vancouver for work. While she's there she's going to file for divorce. I'd begun to think she wouldn't actually go through with it."

Aidan whistled softly through his teeth. "*Now* will you contest it?"

Nate shrugged helplessly. "I have no grounds. But I tell you, I'm not going to find it easy to move on with my life. Last night I had to admit that I wasn't blameless regarding our breakup."

"It's rarely just one person's fault."

But for him to be wrong, oh that hurt. Nate stared moodily into his coffee cup. It had been easier all these years to believe *she* was the whole problem. They still had issues but those might be resolved with a little more effort. The main thing now was that he, Nate, had to redeem himself.

"So what are you going to do?" Aidan said, cutting through Nate's thoughts to the heart of the matter.

Nate lifted his head and stared over the valley. "I'm going to win her back."

CHAPTER NINE

"THANKS TO YOUR EFFORTS, advertising revenue is at an all-time high," Denise Moore, the editorial director at *Businesswoman's Weekly* told Angela at their meeting in Denise's corner office the next day. "Unfortunately, circulation is down for the second quarter in a row. I'm hoping you'll have some fresh ideas."

Angela opened her briefcase and referred to the notes she'd made earlier. "We could try a new layout, look at new retail outlets, maybe redefine our target audience and expand the scope of the magazine."

A burst of laughter outside the office made both women glance over to the door. Denise shrugged and Angela continued. "Articles from recent issues on conference wardrobes and laptop computers look interesting enough but we should be on top of the latest trends. I presume you've discussed this with your editorial staff?"

"Of course," Denise said. "I would have had

you sit in on that meeting but I know it's hard for you to get away.''

Denise had no idea how hard. Angela checked her watch discreetly and wondered what Ricky and Nate were doing right now. *Nate*. She felt good they'd cleared the air about their past. For the first time he'd acknowledged his role in her leaving. But although she'd given him ample opportunity to ask her not to file for divorce, he hadn't. He'd even *reminded* her to take the documents.

The buzz of voices outside erupted in another burst of laughter. ''I wonder what's going on,'' Angela said.

''Probably someone came in with lunch orders,'' Denise suggested. ''The staff goes into a feeding frenzy every day about this time. I'll ask them to pipe down.''

Speaking of lunch, Angela hoped Ricky would remember to eat the sandwich she'd packed for him. Absently she rubbed at a tiny smear of peanut butter on her suit jacket. For some reason she wasn't bothered by it as much as she would have expected. A few weeks with a young boy had de-sensitized her dirt-alert mechanism.

Denise opened the door to the sound of a baby's cry. Sheila, from the art department, and Barbara, from accounts, were clustered around a woman holding a disgruntled-looking baby. All three women began to make soft cooing sounds, and the cry gradually turned to a gurgling chuckle.

"Penny's brought in her new baby," Denise said. "She promised she would."

Angela followed Denise into the open-plan section of the office. Penny's baby was a girl, judging by the pink ribbon circling her round bald head. Now the baby was chortling sweetly in response to tickles under her chin and armpits.

Angela edged closer. "What's her name?"

"Ruby, because she's so precious." Penny beamed adoringly at her daughter.

"She's darling," Angela said. "How old is she?"

"Eight weeks. Would you like to hold her?" Penny placed Ruby in the crook of Angela's arms.

"Oh!" Angela exclaimed at the solid wriggling weight. Ruby settled and Angela stroked a fingertip gently down a soft fat cheek. The infant gurgled and flashed her a gummy grin. Angela's thoughts flashed back to her miscarried pregnancy with a sharp pang. Breathing in the scent of baby powder and innocence she hummed as she rocked gently from side to side and longed for her own lost baby.

"Are you ready to come back to work?" Denise asked Penny. "I'd like to find some way of keeping both you and Angela on board."

"I'm enjoying being at home," Penny said. "But I can't afford to be a full-time mom."

"It can't be easy juggling new motherhood and full-time work," Angela said. "Especially with a new baby."

"It's not, according to my friends who're doing it," Penny told her. "That whole notion of superwoman is a myth. All of the working mothers I know are completely frazzled and more than a few secretly long for the days when women were expected to stay home and raise children. Either that, or they want equal shares in child rearing and housework with their partners."

"Hear, hear," Sheila chimed in. "I take care of *two* babies—my little boy, Tony, and my husband."

"My partner, Derek, works sixty hours a week," Barbara said. "If I have a baby I'll be bringing it up on my own. The nanny and I, that is. Sometimes you wonder what's the point of having children."

"I'm not saying you two are wrong but I'm sure lots of men take an active role in raising their children," Angela said. She couldn't imagine Nate not sharing the tasks as well as the joys of parenthood.

"My husband, Brett, is a wonderful dad," Penny agreed. "But he's simply not home as much as I am and the bulk of child care falls on my shoulders. Not that I'm complaining—I wouldn't have it any other way. I just think the pressure on modern women to do it all—have a family and a career—is too great.''

Angela glanced at Denise, eyebrows raised. "I scent an article in this. What do you think?"

One hand across her waist, the other propping up her chin, Denise narrowed her eyes thoughtfully. "'Motherhood and the Career Woman: Recipe for Oppression?'"

"The title needs work if you don't want to sound too negative," Penny said, laughing. "But the angle is timely."

"Then you'd be willing to collaborate with a writer on this?" Denise said persuasively.

"Sure, I guess." Penny reached for her baby and Angela handed Ruby back reluctantly.

"Let's go to my office and talk about it. Coming, Angela?"

Angela nodded and fell in step. Penny's article might not single-handedly revive circulation but it *was* a fresh angle and that was always good for sales.

It wasn't until the next day at noon that Angela had time to walk from her Denman Street office to the courthouse with the necessary documents in her briefcase. Her feet felt heavy and her steps slowed the nearer she got. She told herself she was just tired, having had a poor sleep the night before. Her immaculate apartment, far from cheering her up, seemed depressingly sterile, and she'd longed for the cheerful clutter of toy cars and family photos.

With all this talk about babies, suddenly she was seeing them everywhere—a tiny face in a stroller, a bobbing head in a baby backpack and a Gerber cherub being spoon-fed in an ad on the side of a bus. Ten years ago she hadn't been ready to have a child. She was now—and she wanted Nate to be the father.

The nearer she got to the courthouse the stronger her conviction became that she didn't want a divorce. The thought of going through with it left her icy even though the rainy period was over and a hot sun was drying the sidewalks and bringing out lunchtime sun bakers on the courthouse lawns. But if Nate hadn't asked her *not* to, what choice did she have? She couldn't stay married to a man who didn't want her.

She found the correct room, told a squat matronly woman her business, and handed over the sheaf of documents.

Pursing her dark red lips the woman checked through the various documents laid out on the counter. "Everything seems to be in order." She started to place the papers into a manila folder.

"What happens next?" Angela inquired dully, even though she knew.

"There's a two-week period during which the application can be appealed, after which the final documents are submitted to the judge who grants the divorce order."

"How long will that take?" Angela's fingers kept straying of their own accord toward the papers as if itching to snatch them back. Finally she put her hand in her pocket.

"Anywhere from three to twelve weeks depending on how busy the courts are." The clerk filed away the documents in the folder. "They've been processing divorces pretty quick lately. You shouldn't have long to wait."

Angela's heart sank. "And once the two-week deadline is passed there's no way my husband can appeal?"

Was it at all possible he would change his mind in time and at least try to stop proceedings? He'd saved her china horses, an unexpected tenderness. He'd admitted he was partly wrong. What else might he be capable of?

The woman smiled reassuringly. "Not a chance." She picked up Angela's file and started to move away. "Have a nice d—"

"Stop!" Angela cried. She leaned over the counter and grabbed at the file folder, getting hold of one corner.

"What are you doing?" Frowning, the woman maintained her grip on the folder.

For one awful moment they had a tug-of-war with the folder, until Angela's greater determination wrested it from the clerk's grasp.

"I've changed my mind," she said, clutching the folder to her chest. "I don't want to go through with it." As she spoke, a huge weight seemed to roll off her shoulders.

"All you had to do was ask and I'd have given you the folder back," the woman sniffed.

"I'm sorry," Angela said, embarrassed. "I truly am. I...I panicked."

"Are you sure you want to withdraw your application for divorce?" The woman lowered her voice and spoke confidentially. "There are support services available, you know. Don't stay with an abusive partner because you're afraid of him."

"He's not abusive. He's a wonderful man. I...I love him. Please, I don't want to go through with the divorce."

Angela shoved the documents back in her briefcase and walked away from the courthouse, lighthearted for the first time in weeks. If Nate wanted a divorce he'd have to get one himself. What *she* wanted was another chance.

But as she drove back to Whistler one question

still niggled her—the chemistry was still there but was the love?

He liked her, judging by the joking camaraderie they shared. He desired her—his hard body in the hot tub had left her in no doubt of that. He must feel connected to her, or he would have asked her for a divorce long ago.

But *love?* Yes, he'd said so but he'd been toying with her. Maybe he wasn't sure she was wife material. After all, she didn't have a very good track record in that department. But she could learn and she was an expert on marketing; she could sell herself as a domestic goddess.

Meanwhile she wouldn't tell Nate she hadn't applied for divorce. Let him sweat it out a little longer.

The sun was still shining when she came to a halt at the stoplights at the entrance to Whistler. High above, the white mountain peaks glistened brightly and the forests cloaking their lower levels were a rich vibrant green.

Angela felt more optimistic than she had in years. Getting on with life had taken on a whole new meaning.

NATE HEARD ANGELA'S FOOTSTEPS on the stairs and went to open the front door. Whenever he saw her he experienced a jolt of attraction but this time he did a complete double take. His gaze swept over her once and then again. She seemed to sparkle all over. "Have you done something to your hair?"

She smiled, her eyes aglow. "No."

"New dress?"

Laughing, she stepped past him, brushing his chest with her shoulder, leaving her scent in his nostrils. "Aren't you going to ask me in?"

"I would but you seem to already be in." Nate followed her into his kitchen. Through the open sliding doors came the sound of a dog's playful bark. "Ricky's in the backyard with Rufus, Mom and Dad's dog."

Angela stepped onto the balcony. "How's Ricky been? Not too much trouble, I hope."

"Nah, he's a great kid." Nate leaned on the railing, watching Ricky throw a ball for a rangy Irish setter whose red coat gleamed and rippled in the sun.

She waved to her nephew. "Hi, Ricky."

Ricky turned to wave back and the dog bounded into him, knocking him to the ground. Boy and dog rolled in the grass like puppies.

"Just think," Nate mused. "If we'd had a kid when we were living together he or she would be about Ricky's age right now. That could be our child out there, playing with the dog."

He hoped she wouldn't construe that as pressure

or anything other than wistful, wishful thinking. Who knows, she might even agree. So he was disappointed when his comment wiped the smile off Angela's face. But only for a moment before she countered his assertion.

"If we'd had a kid back then we wouldn't be the same people we are now. I might not have gone into journalism and you might still be a hammer jockey working for someone else."

"Possibly...I never thought of it that way."

"Well, you should *start* thinking in different ways." Her mood was playful yet forceful. "Turn things around, upside down, and look at them from all angles."

He eyed her curiously. "Did something happen to you in Vancouver? You seem...different."

She cocked her head to the side, chin tilted up. "Same person, new perspective."

"Whatever that means." A chill of foreboding tingled down his spine. Did filing for divorce give a woman this sense of purpose and excitement?

"You'll figure it out in time, I'm sure." She turned to go back into the kitchen and stopped dead at the sight of the kitchen table loaded with crystal wineglasses, vases, three sets of salt-and-pepper shakers and various small appliances. "What's this?"

"Our wedding presents," Nate said. "I decided

it's not fair for me to hog all this stuff. I thought we could go through it and divide it up."

"But that's ridiculous. It's been ten years." The glow enveloping Angela dimmed, like a forty-watt bulb during a brown out. For a moment she just stared at the table and its contents. Then as if coming to some internal conclusion, she straightened her shoulders and showed him her brightest smile. "Or I could move in and use my half here."

"Uh, yeah, I—I—" Nate spluttered. She'd zigged when he'd expected her to zag. But this could turn out even better.

"No, it won't work." She dismissed the idea abruptly before he could agree. "Ricky."

"Oh, right." *Damn.*

She placed two sets of salt-and-pepper shakers to either end of the counter and picked up the third set in both hands. "Which do you want, the salt or the pepper?"

Nate rolled his eyes. *"Angela."*

"Silly, isn't it?" Replacing the shakers she crossed her arms and leveled a firm stare at him. "Where is that photo album? If you want to divvy things up that's the place to start."

"Not the photo album."

She swept past him, through the kitchen and dining room and on into the living room. "On the bookshelf, I think you said."

Nate followed. There was no point resisting when she was in this mood. "Bottom shelf, on the right."

Angela crouched to retrieve the album then retreated to the sofa. She patted the seat beside her. "Come on. The sooner it's over, the better you'll feel."

He doubted that, but he sat next to her anyway. Instead of looking at the photos he admired the graceful way her neck curved into her collarbone. Her golden skin was slightly sunburned across the shoulders with a dusting of pale freckles he didn't remember.

"Remember this day?" she said, nudging him. "We had such a blast."

Nate dragged his gaze to a photo of them and another couple canoeing on Lost Lake shortly after he and Angela had met. The foursome had had a water fight and what he principally remembered about that day—besides Angela's wet T-shirt plastered to her breasts—was her unflappable good humor and the way they'd worked together as a team. "Mind if I keep this?"

"Okay, but I want this one." She pointed to a photo taken at a barbecue at his parents' place. Aidan and Marc were there plus some of the Wilde cousins from Vancouver Island. Angela was sitting on the picnic table and Nate was standing beside her, his arm casually draped around her shoulders. "Look at our faces."

Her eyes were half-closed and dreamy and his smile resembled that of the proverbial cat who ate the canary.

"You recall why we looked like that, don't you?" he said, turning to her.

She blushed a deep rose color. "'Come up and see my biking trophies before dinner.' Honestly, Nate."

"I thought it was pretty original. It worked, didn't it?"

"Only because we were already married." She slid the photo from its sleeve and set it aside.

The empty space looked lonely to Nate and he quickly moved on. "I guess you'll want this one," he said, indicating a photo of Angela and Janice standing beside the bike trail on Whistler to watch him race. The next photo, a blur in a cloud of dust, he supposed was himself.

"Thanks. You can have this, and this…all of these." She flipped over a page of photos of different mountain bikes. "Ohh." A sigh escaped her.

Nate leaned forward to see what she was looking at. It was a close-up of them on the top of Whistler Mountain with snow-covered peaks in the background. A strand of hair had blown across Angela's face but it didn't obscure her luminous smile or the sparkle in her eyes. *He* looked filled to bursting with pride and happiness, as if he'd have floated right off the mountain if she hadn't been holding his hand.

He would remember that afternoon forever. In their special place on the secluded knoll, he'd proposed and she'd said yes.

The silence stretched, crowded with memories and emotions. Nate realized they'd leaned together on the sofa when he felt the warmth where they were touching at the thigh and shoulder.

He eased back a little and cleared his throat. "This was taken near the chairlift after we'd hiked back from our spot. I can't recall—who snapped the picture?"

"A tourist who happened to be passing." She made a small sound in her throat, halfway between a sob and a sigh. "Nate, I want this photo."

"I want it, too."

They twisted to face each other. Her jaw was set and her gaze determined. Nate knew she could be as stubborn as he was at times. Splitting up their photos was stupid. If the pictures still meant so much to them they should stay together.

"There's only one way to solve this," he said grimly, sliding the photo out of the plastic sleeve.

"What are you doing?" Angela reached for the photo but he twisted away, quickly folding it in half and tearing along the crease. Oh!'' she gasped and began to pummel him on the chest, raging, ''Why did you do that?''

Nate tossed down the torn halves of the photo and gripped her wrists to stop her from hitting him. Blue eyes blazing, she struggled but was no match for his superior strength.

Nate bent his head and kissed her.

She ceased fighting immediately and put her arms around his neck, kissing him back in a way that made his blood roar in his veins and left him dizzy. He didn't know what had gotten into her but he wasn't arguing. Wanting more, he crushed her to him. His onslaught overbalanced her and she fell back, pulling him down on top of her. A haze of desire obliterated everything but the honey taste of her lips, the exquisite torture of her soft curves—

''Hey, Nate!'' a young voice called faintly from outside. ''Can Rufus and me have a drink?''

Footsteps stumping up the stairs accompanied by the scrabble of paws on wooden steps penetrated Nate's brain. He sat up, pulling Angela with him. She looked as stunned as he felt, shoving her hair into place and tugging on her blouse.

''Sorry,'' Nate said. ''I don't know what came over me.''

''I do,'' Angela replied. ''It's called lust.''

''Shh. Here's Ricky.'' Nate got up and went to

meet the boy in the kitchen and poured him a glass
of juice.

"Thanks. Where's Angela?"

"Here I am." Angela appeared in the doorway,
collected and calm. "Drink up. It's time we went
home."

Ricky drank steadily, a tiny frown of concentration between his eyebrows. Nate met Angela's
gaze over the boy's blond head. His pretence of
dividing up their wedding gifts had been formu-
lated to jolt her into considering what she was doing to the pair of them but the turn of events had
ended up shocking him.

She gave him a serene smile as if to say she
hadn't been affected nearly as much as he'd like
to think. Then she surprised him by saying, "Can
you come over for dinner on Saturday, Nate?"

"Are you…?"

"Cooking? Yes." She seemed vexed when he
hesitated. "Nothing frozen, nothing takeout, I
promise you."

"Thanks, I'd like that." *I think.*

"Good. Ricky, go get your overnight bag. No,
doggy, you're not coming with us."

"Out, Rufus." Nate shooed him back through
the sliding door and shut it. Turning to Angela, he
asked, "Did you get your photos?"

"Yes, and I took half of the one you tore up." She shook her head. "You are so hotheaded."

Not *that* hotheaded; he had the negative. "Maybe you don't know me as well as you think you do."

"Hmm, you could be right. Ah, there you are, Ricky. Say 'thank you' to Nate."

"Thank-you-for-having-me," Ricky recited in the robotic voice peculiar to children whose parents have drilled the niceties into them.

"Anytime, dude." Nate walked them to the door. "See you Saturday."

He watched while they got in the green Dodge and drove away, emitting a puff of black smoke, then went back to the living room to put the photos away, trying not to look at the empty slots in the pages. *Now* he felt separated. The torn half of the photo was upside down. He turned it over, wondering whose picture she'd chosen to keep.

Angela's radiant smile beamed up at him.

CHAPTER TEN

"COFFEE OR TEA?" Leone asked when the kettle had boiled. "I'm drinking green tea these days, myself."

"Green tea is fine for me, too." Angela sat on a bar stool at the kitchen counter. Sunlight streamed through the sliding-glass doors to pool onto terra-cotta tiles and the big red dog at her feet. A plate of brownies sat next to her elbow, tempting her.

"What did you want to see me so urgently about?" Leone asked when a few minutes later she poured Angela a cup of straw-colored tea and pushed the plate of brownies under her nose.

"I'm cooking dinner for Nate and I need to know his favorite meal." Angela bit into a brownie. "I hope it's cake. This is delicious."

"Nate isn't much of one for sweets. I thought you would have known that."

"I've never been much of one for cooking. I thought you would have known *that*."

"I guess I did." Leone reached down to stroke

Rufus, who had moved to her side. Her head tilted delicately, she said, "May I ask what prompted this foray into domesticity?"

"I, uh, just want to thank him for looking after Ricky while I was in Vancouver," Angela said.

"Ricky's such a sweet boy," Leone said. "How are his mother and father doing in Europe? Have you heard from them?"

Angela chatted about her sister's adventures in France and Germany for a few minutes before bringing the subject back to Nate's favorite meal.

"He loves my cabbage rolls and he used to be partial to pot roast," Leone said. "Since he's been cooking for himself he goes in mainly for seafood and fresh vegetables. No heavy fried food, that's certain."

Angela sipped her slightly bitter tea and contemplated a future without French fries. For Nate she was willing to give them up. But not chocolate. Or pizza.

"I could make him a salad," she said, considering the matter. "Although that doesn't seem very impressive."

"I know just the thing." Leone jumped up and went to a glass-and-chrome bookshelf at one end of the family room. Taking down a large cookbook she laid it in front of Angela. "Nate gave me this last Christmas. The dear boy meant well, but I've never cooked a single one of the recipes."

The cookbook was California fusion—a blend of western and Asian influences. Angela leafed through the pages, pausing to study a luscious-looking photo of a mixed seafood grill and colorful vegetables on a wide white plate. How hard could this be? "May I borrow this cookbook?"

"Keep it as long as you like. If you get stuck, give me a call and I'll try to help," Leone said, friendly enough but with that touch of reserve she'd had ever since Angela had returned to Whistler.

Angela drained her tea and said, "I'd better go. You probably have a lot to do seeing as it's your day off."

When Leone didn't make even a token protest Angela hesitated, loathe to leave on cool terms. "I really wish marriage had turned out differently for Nate and I," she began, struggling to find the words and the breath to speak them. Leone regarded her patiently. "A lot of it was my fault and this dinner is my way of trying to make up for it. I…I'm hoping Nate and I will eventually get back together."

"Oh, my dear." Shiny eyed, Leone leaned over and embraced her in a warm hug. "I'm so glad to hear you say that. I hope so, too."

"Thank you." Angela blinked rapidly. "But please don't say anything to Nate or...or anyone, even Jim. Nate and I need to work out our problems in our own way, in our own time. I'm not even sure he'll want to get back together and it would be so embarrassing if—"

"Don't even think that," Leone admonished. "But I promise I won't say anything."

Angela gave Leone another hug. "I'll let you know how it turns out."

Angela picked up Ricky then drove through a fast-food outlet for two orders of hamburgers, French fries and chocolate shakes to go. Tomorrow was soon enough to start her healthy-eating kick.

That night she spent a couple of hours knitting Nate's sweater while watching TV with Ricky. During commercial breaks Ricky filled her in on his activities over the past two days.

"Sounds like you had a good time with Nate." She flipped her circular needles around to start another row, adding, "Don't pick at your scab."

Ricky, who was lying on his stomach on the carpeted floor, dropped his hand away from his forehead guiltily. "He showed me how to predict the weather and everything." He glanced up at her curiously. "Hey, how come there are pictures on his wall of you in a wedding dress standing next to him? Are you guys married?"

Angela slipped a stitch, cursed softly and fumbled with the needles, trying to pick it up. Finally, she put the knitting in her lap and looked at Ricky. "We *were* married a long time ago, before you were born."

"How come you're not married now?"

She considered the many complicated reasons and explanations she might give and decided Ricky didn't really want to know all that. "Technically, we're just separated. I went back East and he stayed here."

"How come you don't live together now?"

"Um, I'm staying here to take care of you."

"Oh." Ricky accepted that without a quibble, possibly because the TV program had come on again.

Angela counted her stitches and found she now had one too many. When she'd rectified the matter, she said casually, "Why didn't you ask Nate?"

"Huh?" Ricky took his gaze off the screen long enough to throw a quick glance over his shoulder. "Oh, I did but he said only you knew the answer to those questions."

Angela snorted. "Coward," she muttered.

"Pardon?"

"Nothing."

Half an hour later, when Angela thought Ricky had long forgotten the issue, he rolled on his back and squinted at the ceiling through his fingers. "It'd be cool if you got married to him again. Then Nate would be my uncle and you would live here all the time."

Angela smiled and said nothing. *Fingers crossed, it would happen.*

The next day she spent the morning running around Whistler searching out ingredients for the dish she'd picked out of Leone's cookbook. Luckily the resort was cosmopolitan and catered to many Japanese tourists; she had no trouble finding everything she needed.

When she was ready, Angela donned an apron and lined up the ingredients on the kitchen counter: wasabi paste, pickled ginger, dashi fish stock, Japanese eggplant, tofu, nori seaweed and—shudder— fresh squid.

Nate loved seafood. This would be a meal he'd never forget and would launch her reputation as a domestic goddess. Kerry Martin, move over.

Sometime later she realized to her chagrin that actually making the dish was trickier than she'd thought.

To remove the slender piece of cartilage known as the pen, tug lightly, being careful not to break the ink sac—

She pulled on the slippery pen, her nails digging into the squid for grip. Brown liquid squirted from the punctured ink sac. *Ugh.* Sepia was everywhere, on the benchtop, the cookbook and the brand-new apron Angela'd bought for the occasion. Grinding her teeth, she sponged off the ink.

Hours later Ricky bounded into the kitchen. ''When's dinner going to be ready? I'm starving.''

Angela glanced at the clock and saw with a sinking heart that she only had thirty minutes before Nate was to arrive. So much for her visions of a relaxing scented bath and an hour primping in front of the mirror while dinner simmered on the stove. ''You'd better make yourself a peanut-butter sandwich. There's no telling when this will be ready.''

Or if it would be edible. But she didn't say that. Best not to jinx herself.

''Would you like to go for a bike ride tomorrow?'' Angela added as Ricky got out the bread and peanut butter.

''Just you and me?'' Ricky glanced around in surprise and dropped a dollop of peanut butter on the counter. Angela bit her tongue. Who was she to complain about a mess?

''Yes.'' She waited anxiously for his answer. Maybe he wouldn't want to go with his aunt. Maybe he'd want to bring Tim—

''Cool! That would be fun.'' Ricky's generous smile was so thoroughly accepting she came over and hugged him, marveling at the strength in his skinny young body. He hugged her back, clinging a second longer than necessary.

"I'm so glad I came to stay with you," she whispered, smoothing his hair from his forehead. Now she'd embarrassed him and he squirmed out of her arms. Smiling, Angela watched him run outside, his sandwich clutched in his grubby hand.

Eventually she got the cartilaginous pens out of all the squid and rinsed the ink off herself and all washable surfaces. Pity about Janice's tea towels. Then she turned to the stuffing ingredients. Uh-oh. She was supposed to cook the eggplant *before* stuffing the squid. Why hadn't the recipe mentioned that right up front? Did the cookbook author expect people to read the recipe all the way through before starting?

Come to think of it, that might not be a bad idea in the future. Apparently she was supposed to salt the eggplant and let it sit for thirty minutes before cooking. She cast a desperate glance at the clock. Time was fast running out.

She cut the salting time to twenty minutes and zapped the eggplant in the microwave to hasten the cooking. Even then the whole process was taking far too long and the brown-and-purple mush that resulted hardly seemed worth the effort. Still she persevered.

To the cooked eggplant she added grated fresh

ginger, sesame oil and a tablespoon of wasabi paste. Only one tablespoon? It looked so bland, why not two? Oh, what the heck, make it *four* tablespoons. Cooking was supposed to be creative, and the green contrasted prettily with the deep purple of the eggplant—even though the paste made her eyes water. She stuffed the eggplant mixture into the cavity of the flaccid gray squid, trying not to shudder at the cold rubbery texture of the flesh. Ugh, it was falling out. She picked it up and jammed it back in, securing the ends with toothpicks that kept breaking. At last she got the squid into the baking dish and into the oven.

Now for the appetizers. These proved to be fiddly and time consuming and she had to improvise again, but eventually she stood back and surveyed her creation proudly. She was adding the finishing touches when the doorbell rang.

Angela rinsed her hands under the tap, tucked a loose strand of hair behind her ear and hurried to the door.

Nate, standing on the porch with a bottle of wine in one hand and flowers in the other, heard her footsteps. *No matter how sexy she is, stay cool. Pay her a compliment. Woo her.*

The door opened. Angela, her hair tousled, her apron daubed with blobs of unidentifiable goop and a near hysterical glint in her eyes, looked like an explosives expert whose luck had run out. Nate sniffed the air discreetly, trying to determine whether the peculiar aroma emanating from the kitchen was dangerous or merely dinner.

He decided diplomacy was the better part of valor. "Uh, hi," he said. "You look…nice."

"Don't be funny." Her gaze fell on the wine bottle with the desperation of an alcoholic. "You'd better open that now. You look like you need a drink."

"I feel quite certain I'm going to," he said faintly.

Nate followed her to the kitchen where she stopped abruptly on the threshold and turned to him with a terse, "Don't say anything."

He obeyed, mainly because the sight that met his eyes rendered him speechless. Every counter was cluttered with open jars, dirty dishes and bits of unidentifiable food, a good deal of which was on the floor. The pantry door hung open, the contents all jumbled. Every dish and pan in the house appeared to have been used and stacked higgledy-piggledy in the sink.

"I wouldn't come any farther if I were you," Angela warned. "It's not safe." She picked her way across the grimy floor, rummaged in the top drawer for a corkscrew then reached into an upper cupboard for two wineglasses.

Nate took the corkscrew from her and went back into the living room to open the wine. Angela noticed she still had on her filthy apron and with a grimace of disgust, took it off and tossed it into the laundry. She came back out, running her hands through her hair to tame it. He handed her a glass of wine. She drank it down in one long gulp, blotted her mouth with the back of her hand and extended the glass for a refill.

"Rough day?" he essayed.

"The worst." She sank into the couch and sipped at her second glass of wine. "How about you?"

"Mine was okay."

She nodded, further words apparently beyond her. Then her eyes closed and she was silent so long he began to wonder if she'd fallen asleep. He was just about to remove the glass from her hand before it spilled when her eyes suddenly snapped open. "Ricky."

"He's playing out front with the boy across the street," Nate told her, deducing she was worried about her nephew's whereabouts and general safety.

A long low sigh eased from her flared nostrils as her shoulders relaxed and dropped lower. She took another sip of wine. "Are you hungry?"

''So-so.'' He waggled his hand cautiously. ''When will dinner be ready?''

Lifting her arm as if it were a dead weight she checked her watch. ''Oh, I'd say…ten o'clock.'' Then she began to giggle.

Nate took the glass from her hand and set it on the table. ''We'd better pace ourselves.''

His stomach rumbled and he clamped a hand over it, as if that would muffle the sound. ''Excuse me. It's been a while since lunch.''

''Never fear,'' Angela said, brightening. ''I have appetizers.''

She went back to the kitchen and returned with a platter of thin rice crackers topped with a scraping of what looked like putty garnished with translucent slivers of green. *''Ta da,''* she sang. ''Tofu and kelp crackers.''

Nate gulped. ''This'll keep me going.''

She watched him closely, seeming pleased by his enthusiasm. ''It's my own recipe.''

Nate popped a cracker whole into his mouth and chewed. Years of playing poker with Aidan and Marc paid off as he struggled to keep his expression blank. ''There's another flavor…I can't quite place it.''

''Honey and mustard sauce. I spread it below the tofu. White food always seems so bland, don't you think?''

Nate swallowed but the taste lingered unpleasantly on his tongue. "Very, er, innovative."

Angela bit into a cracker and made a face. She chewed bravely for a moment then, holding a hand to her mouth, got up and ran from the room. Nate could hear the sounds of spitting in the bathroom down the corridor. Quickly he gathered up five or six of the crackers, folded them into a napkin and stuffed them in his pocket.

When Angela returned he rubbed his stomach and gave her what he hoped was a sheepish smile. "They were so good I ate most of them."

She looked at the platter, eyed him suspiciously, then offered him a second helping.

His hand shot up, palm out. "Thanks, but I couldn't eat another one. They're very filling."

Mollified, she set the platter down again. "If you liked those, you'll love the main course."

"I can't wait." This time Nate's smile was more a baring of the teeth in anticipation of further torture.

By the time they ate, Ricky had long gone to bed. Angela had set the table, put Nate's flowers in a vase and lit the candles on a linen-covered dining table. The setting seemed pitched for romance. Nate played with his water glass, wondering what her game was. She'd resisted all his attempts at seduction, oblique as they were, and now *this?* On the other hand, the low lighting might not mean she had romance on her mind but more a desire to disguise the main course.

She brought out a long flat casserole dish and served him something resembling a miniature Beluga whale. It quivered as she passed him the plate and he felt the remnants of tofu, mustard and honey rise in his throat.

"It looks delicious," he said gamely. "What do you call it?"

"I called it all sorts of things while I was making it." Angela gazed dubiously at her own plate. "The recipe is for stuffed squid."

"I like squid," he said truthfully. "Although I didn't think it took that long to cook." In fact, he couldn't think of *anything* that took four hours to bake.

"It looked so wiggly and alive when it was raw," Angela told him. "I wanted to make sure it was dead."

Nate started to slice off a bite. The knife pressed into, but didn't penetrate, the rubbery surface. Next he tried a sawing motion which after a minute or so of steady labor yielded a bite-size corner he jammed onto his fork. The stuffing, a bilious mixture of purple and green fell out with a wet plop. Dutifully he scooped it back onto his fork and pushed the whole thing into his mouth.

It was like eating fire and the fire hose at the same time; the stuffing was spicy hot and the squid tough and rubbery. He chewed doggedly, keeping his mouth closed by dint of great determination while his eyes watered and his sinuses drained in his body's attempt to douse the invading flames.

By this time, Angela had sawn off a bite of her own and popped it into her mouth. With a screech she once again ran from the room and slammed the door on the bathroom.

She was gone a long time and when she returned her face was very pale. "I'm so sorry. This dinner is a disaster!" Then she sank onto her chair and buried her face in her hands. Her shoulders began to heave and muffled sounds emerged from behind her hands.

Nate watched her for a moment, feeling sorry for her disappointment after all the effort she'd obviously put into dinner. He leaned over and put a hand on her shoulder. "Don't cry, Ange." Angela peered through splayed fingers with moist red eyes. "If you scrape out the stuffing the squid doesn't taste too bad," he added. Then her hands fell away to reveal a wide grin; her shoulders were shaking with laughter, not tears. Nate shook his head in indignation. "I'm glad you think it's funny that I burned my mouth and risked terminal indigestion trying to eat your cooking."

"Oh, Nate," she gasped, unable to control her mirth. "Sorry. I'm feeling a little hysterical. I wasn't laughing at you but at this revolting meal. Have you ever tasted anything so unbearably awful?"

Nate had to smile. One thing he'd always loved about Angela was her ability to laugh at herself. "Actually, no, but I was going to be polite and not mention it."

"You're a saint…" His stomach rumbled loudly and she went into another fit of the giggles. "That dinner was so bad a starving dog wouldn't touch it."

Her merriment was contagious. "That dinner was so bad," he said, snorting, "they'd turn it away from the garbage dump."

Angela shrieked. "That dinner was so bad Saddam Hussein could have used it to torture his enemies."

Nate's sides had begun to hurt but he couldn't stop his compulsive chuckling. "That dinner was so bad it could be grounds for divorce—" He broke off.

Angela wasn't laughing anymore.

His smile faded, leaving behind sore cheeks and a bad feeling in his stomach that had nothing to do with her food. "I meant that as a joke."

"It's okay." She sniffed, and rose to clear away

the uneaten portions. ''Think what you've been spared these past ten years.''

''Angela.'' He reached for her arm but she pulled away.

''Don't worry. I'll do better next time.''

''Next time!'' he repeated in alarm.

She threw him a laughing glance over her shoulder. ''Gotcha!''

The defrosted and reheated enchiladas Angela brought out next were more successful than the meal she'd slaved over all day. The knowledge was galling but maybe she'd do better at housework. Lord knows, she was going to get a chance to practice when she tackled the kitchen.

They left the mess on the dining table and took their plates to the couch, eating hungrily and silently, every now and then meeting each other's eyes. Occasionally Nate's knee touched hers and the tiny circle of contact spread warmth right through her. She felt as though she was nineteen again, on the steps of the hotel, gazing into the eyes of a man she'd thought she could only dream about having.

At last she set her empty plate on the coffee table. ''Thanks for being such a good sport about dinner.''

''We Wildes are known for our adventurous spirit,'' he said, smiling. ''You were brave, too, to attempt such a difficult recipe. Next time try something simpler, like Duck à L'Orange.'' She looked at him uncertainly and he added, ''I'm joking.''

Nate edged closer and wrapped his warm fingers around hers to lift her bent knuckles to his lips. His mouth on her skin made her feel breathless. She was tempted to let their instincts determine what happened next but that wasn't her way.

Angela took a deep breath. ''You were right when you said we still had chemistry. Unfortunately it's not enough to build a marriage on.''

He turned her hand over and unfurled her fingers to kiss her open palm. ''What would *you* build a marriage on—trust?''

She winced. He was making her want him and at the same time reminding her of why he'd kept his distance. She tugged her hand away. ''Sex, trust, both those, but more important, knowing the other person.''

Nate eased back to an upright position. ''Are you saying we don't know each other?''

''That's right. We got married not only too young, but too quickly. We didn't have time to find out where we stood on important issues before they became the wedge that drove us apart.''

Nate looked unconvinced. ''We did get married quickly but I believe you know when a person's right for you.''

"Maybe that's true but now we're stuck in a place where it's difficult to get past the old hurts and resentments. I propose we forget our early days and look at each other with fresh eyes…see if we still have anything in common. Anything worth pursuing."

"Pity this didn't occur to you before you filed for divorce," he said dryly.

Avoiding his gaze, she said, "Best-laid plans, and all that." Her hands started to twist together and she forced herself to hold them still. *Don't let him see how vulnerable you are.* Big breath in, big breath out. Look up. Smile. "So what do you say? Do you want to give it the old college try one more time? For the Gipper?"

"Just exactly what are you proposing? We're still married, technically speaking. Making love would be perfectly legitimate."

"I don't think we should cloud our minds with the physical side of a relationship, at least not yet," she said. "We know we could jump into bed at the drop of a hat. But can we have a real conversation, one that lasts for more than the space of a television commercial?"

Nate began to look truly interested. "I'd like to find out."

"I'll bet if we took the time to really get to know each other instead of resorting to verbal jousting we'd discover all sorts of interesting things.''

"We just might at that," he said, gazing at her thoughtfully. "I have a suggestion. Why not break completely out of our groove so we're not tempted to fall into the trap of arguing about the past?"

"How do we do that?" she asked.

"Let's meet somewhere as strangers. You know that old trick—you'll be sitting in a bar and I'll come along and ask to buy you a drink. We'll talk, get to know each other, maybe have dinner. If things work out, we'll arrange to go on a real date."

"That sounds like fun. I'll wear a red dress." A spark flared in his eyes, thrilling her right down to her toes. "How will I know *you?*" she asked demurely.

"When I pursue a woman she has no doubt in her mind who I am or what I'm after." He leaned forward, his fingers brushing her jaw as he lifted her chin and bore down with his mouth.

"No kissing." She leaped off the couch just in time, her heart beating wildly. "We haven't even had our first date."

Nate laughed, and rose, too. "If I have to be good, I'd better be gone." He picked up his jacket off the arm of the couch and walked to the door. There he turned, and with an odd enigmatic expression, said, "You do realize that if we fall in love we'll have so much more to lose?"

"Or gain," she said bravely.

He held her gaze for two beats of her heart. "Until tomorrow, then. I'll be at La Bocca Restaurant at seven."

CHAPTER ELEVEN

LA BOCCA WAS NEARLY FULL when Nate arrived at fifteen minutes before seven the next night. Sliding onto a padded leather stool at the bar he glanced around. Red-leather booths on opposite sides of the restaurant separated a dozen or so tables and chairs in a central dining area that gave onto an open courtyard overlooking the Village Square. The taupe stucco walls were embedded with iridescent fragments of cloth or paper, he couldn't tell which, and potted greenery softened the faux stone banked around the bar and cashier's desk. Quiet jazzy piano music tinkled softly over the speakers, just audible above the low buzz of conversation.

"What can I get you, sir?" The bartender, in white shirt and waistcoat, wiped the counter in front of Nate and slid across a bowl of pretzels.

"Bourbon on the rocks, please." A little false courage before "the lady in red" arrived might quell the unexpected flutter in his stomach. He sipped his drink compulsively and watched the door like a guard dog on patrol. Tonight was flavored with the mystery and expectation reminiscent of their courting days, that brief period when their future was unknown but rife with potential.

Angela walked out of the warm summer twilight and into the bar, swaying sexily in a deep red dress that clung to her breasts and hips. Nate's hand froze bringing his glass to his mouth. Her detached gaze met his for an instant, then flickered away. Far from putting him off, her apparent disinterest fueled his competitive instincts. Especially when he saw other men's heads swivel after her as she moved through the room.

Nate turned his back on her and watched her approach through the mirror behind the bar. Cool as a mountain stream, she slid onto a bar stool leaving an empty seat between them. Her eyes met his in the mirror with a faint smile such as a woman might give an attractive stranger.

Shifting her attention to the bartender, she said, "Strawberry margarita, please."

She toyed with a cardboard coaster, deliberately not noticing him, which left Nate free to study her. Her normally smooth blond hair had a tousled look suggestive of pillows and moonlight. Even her voice when she'd asked for her drink sounded softer and lower in register. Sexier. If that was even possible with Angela.

In the mirror Nate spotted a lounge lizard making his way purposefully toward the bar and decided not to wait any longer to make his move. "Is this seat taken?" he asked Angela, indicating the empty stool between them.

Her eyes warmer, she shook her head. "Be my guest."

Casually, he slid over and rested one elbow on the bar as he half turned toward her. "My name's Nate."

"Angela."

"Pretty name. You *look* like an angel. But I bet you get that all the time."

"Not so much." A small smile played over her glistening red lips. "Most guys are more original."

"I'm not very good at pickup lines," he admitted. "I prefer playing it straight."

"Tell me something honest."

Turning to face her straight on, he rested his jaw on his knuckles and thought a moment before replying. "You look like someone I could spend a lot of time with."

She held his gaze over her frothy pink drink. "You look like someone too attractive to be alone."

"I had a wife once." Nate swirled his drink, making the ice cubes clink. "She left me."

"Do you miss her?" She was watching him curiously.

Nate nodded. It was a huge admission for him.

When he'd suggested meeting this way he'd half expected them to treat it like a game and role-play their younger selves as grown-ups. Now he realized that's what they'd been doing all along till now. Tonight felt more real in some ways. And scarier because of that. "What do you do for fun, Angela?"

She stirred her drink. "I knit—"

"Knit! I didn't know—I mean, interesting. I thought only little old ladies knitted. Are you making an afghan?" His mother made afghan quilts; he had three of them.

Laughing, she shook her head. "I'm making a sweater for a friend. Oh, and I've just taken up mountain biking."

"How do you like that?" He could sit here all night asking her questions just to watch the sparkle in her eyes.

"I love it!"

"*Love* it? Really? We're being honest, remember."

"It's true." She swiveled to face him and pulled her dress up to show him a scrape on her thigh. "See? Proof."

As far as Nate was concerned the only thing

she'd proved was that she had the best legs he'd ever seen. "Where'd you get that?"

"I went down a trail I wasn't supposed to go on. I shouldn't have done it, but…well, if you want to know the truth, the instructor was acting like a jerk." Her eyes gleamed mischievously.

One side of his mouth twisted up. "Go on."

"I'd had a hard time learning how to ride—I couldn't even bunny hop, for goodness' sake. But I was furious and I just took off. Not until I was zooming downhill out of control did something click. I heard his voice inside my head. Suddenly I could do all the things I'd been taught but never mastered. The exhilaration, the feeling of accomplishment, was indescribable."

"I know what you mean." In hindsight he could recall the incandescent grin on her face when he'd come upon her in the clearing. She'd tried to tell him then but he'd been full of self-righteous anger and given her hell instead. "You're right, your instructor sounds like a jerk."

"He's not so bad." Angela took a pretzel from the bowl. "Tell me something about yourself."

In other words, something she didn't know. "I'm writing a book on mountain biking."

"So I was ri—" She stopped herself. "How fascinating."

"I haven't told many people about it yet," he

said, guessing from her aborted comment she'd seen his notes beside the computer. "I've never tackled anything like this before."

"I'd love to read it when it's done. Is it about the Whistler area?"

"All over British Columbia. I'm working with a buddy who wrote an earlier edition. I'm updating his material and adding my own descriptions of new trails. I've done all the legwork and now I'm putting together the text."

"Have you got a publisher?" He nodded. "When you're done let me know," she said. "I could help you with some marketing strategies."

"I'd appreciate that." He signaled the bartender for another drink, then reached for her hand where it rested on the bar. "Would you like to join me for dinner? *Angela.*"

Angela, her heart beating rapidly, nodded. He'd done it again—got her with just the way he said her name. Low and sexy but with total respect. She glanced at his fingers tangled in hers then back to his eyes. She was seeing a different side of Nate tonight, one she liked very much. "Do you think we can get a table?"

"I've got one booked out on the terrace." He glanced at his watch. "It should be ready now."

They strolled through the open bifold doors onto the outdoor eating area. The maître d' led them to a table on the edge of the terrace, directly over-looking the square where a string quartet played for tourists in the deepening twilight. The maître d' lit the low candle and discreetly backed away.

Lulled by the romantic setting, Angela sighed.

"What are you thinking?" Nate asked.

"How far I've come." Keeping up the fiction they were strangers, she added, "I used to work at that hotel opposite as a chambermaid and dream that one day I'd be eating in this restaurant just like one of the rich tourists." She toyed with the ceramic saltshaker. "What were *your* dreams when you were young?"

He swirled the drink in his hand. "My dreams always centered around two things—what I could achieve, and who I shared my life with."

"Pity your wife was so unaccommodating," she murmured.

An awkward silence fell until she asked, "Have you always been adventurous?"

He nodded. "When I was laid up with an illness as a child I used to pour over the atlas and wonder about every speck in the ocean—who lived there and what kind of place it was. Nowadays I explore the mountains and forests."

Their conversation drifted from topic to topic almost effortlessly. Nate had more diverse interests than the young man she'd married and he elaborated on them with enthusiasm. She, in turn, found herself telling him more about herself than she'd ever revealed to anyone. Was it the pseudoanonymity of the situation they'd created, or had they broken through to a new level of intimacy? Still, she found it somewhat disconcerting to pretend he was a stranger all the while knowing he had a scar to the right of his tailbone.

Angela was watching his mouth as he talked when the saltshaker slipped from her grasp and fell over, spilling fine white grains across the linen tablecloth. Absently she pinched a bit of salt between her fingers and tossed it over her shoulder.

Nate stopped speaking abruptly. ''Were you always superstitious?''

''You mean the salt? Yes.'' Slipping out of her role, she added, ''There was a lot you didn't notice about me back then.''

''Was I that self-absorbed?''

She shrugged. ''You were a typical twenty-year-old alpha male.''

Nate winced at the harsh but accurate assessment. ''I hope I've changed for the better in the intervening years.''

The waiter came by with a basket of sourdough rolls and a chilled bottle of water with a sprig of fresh mint floating inside. He filled their glasses while rattling off the chef's specials. They ordered food and wine and settled back in their chairs.

"So far we've just skimmed the surface." Nate reached for a roll and began to butter it. "What hits you where you live? What do you hate more than anything?"

Trust him to ask a question that would make her squirm. "You first," she said, stalling.

"Being beaten in a competition," he replied without hesitation. "Your turn."

"Breaking a nail right before an important meeting."

"Ange."

"Okay, so I was being facetious. What I really hate is when the store is out of my favorite flavor of ice cream."

Nate's eyes narrowed and he jabbed his knife in her direction. "I withdraw that question and submit another. Why do you get flippant whenever you feel threatened?"

She started fiddling with the saltshaker again until Nate took it out of her hands. He touched her chin, trying to get her to look at him but her gaze skittered away.

"You wanted us to get to know each other," he reminded her.

"Oh, all right." Her sigh came from the depths. They were playing for keeps. If she wanted to win big, she had to gamble big. "But I warn you, the answer to both your questions is going to sound stupid and trivial."

"Whatever it is, I'll understand."

Somehow she doubted it. Nate was a strong person; he liked having strong people around him. Look at *his* answer, being bested in a competition. It was like being generous to a fault, which was hardly a fault at all. When she told him, he might think of her differently. She'd no longer be the confident carefree woman he'd once been attracted to. But he was waiting for her to open up to him and he wasn't going to go away.

She sucked in a breath and on the exhalation let out a stream of words. "I hate being forgotten, overlooked, discounted, treated as if I didn't matter. There, that's it."

Nate stared at her and drummed his fingers on the tablecloth. "Are you talking about when you left and I didn't come after you?"

"That night triggered feelings from the past but no, this started on my seventh birthday." She could feel her voice on the verge of wavering so she waited until she could speak with hard-edged carelessness. "The year I turned seven my mom forgot my birthday. I'd wanted a Barbie doll because all my friends had one. I didn't get it, end of story. I told you it was trivial."

"When you say she forgot your birthday, do you mean she simply didn't get you a present? Maybe she couldn't afford a Barbie doll."

"It wasn't just the doll. She forgot my birthday completely. No card, no cake, no presents of any kind. *Nothing.*" Angela stopped speaking abruptly as the crushing sense of abandonment flooded back. Her mother was long dead; she had to let this go.

"But *why?*" Nate asked. "How could she forget her own child's birthday?"

She wished he would just leave it alone. Angela shrugged. "I don't know."

"Did Janice remember your birthday?"

"She was only five."

"What about your father? Did he remember?"

"Nope." It came out in a tiny voice. A child's voice.

She cleared her throat. "It was a long time ago. It doesn't matter anymore."

Looking bewildered, Nate took her hand across the table and held it between both of his. "It mattered at the time. Kids take things like that hard. I don't know what to say except I'm sorry." He paused. "Tell me, how does this tie in with you making flippant remarks?"

"When my school friends asked me what I got for my birthday, I made some smart-ass remark about a roomful of Barbie dolls and accessories.'' Angela managed a brilliant, brittle smile. "Ta da, my defense mechanism was born.''

"I had such a different childhood compared to what you went through,'' Nate mused. "My birthday is in August so after my party Dad would take me, Aidan and Marc camping and fishing. I've always looked forward to the time when I would do those things with my kids.''

They were straying into dangerous territory. Angela tried to imagine herself saying, "You would have had a kid ten years ago if I hadn't run off and had a miscarriage,'' and couldn't. She and Nate had achieved a greater degree of closeness tonight but she was sure such news would shatter their rapport. Yet how could they have a future if she wasn't completely honest about the past?

Massaging her forehead between her eyebrows she said, "Can we please not talk about birthdays anymore?''

"Sorry. That was thoughtless of me right after what you told me. Let's do another question. How about—'' He grinned. "What's your worst fault?''

"Boy, you really pick them, don't you?'' she scolded, but was relieved to return to a lighter topic. "Do you honestly think I'm going to tell you my faults?''

"Come on. Don't be shy.''

"No way," she said, shaking her head. "For me to know and you to find out."

He smiled modestly. "I don't have any faults, either."

"You do, too!" She wagged a finger at him, quoting, "'Pride goeth before a fall.'"

Nate flicked a hand in the air as though shooing away a pesky insect. "Pride is a good thing. Everyone should be proud of their abilities and accomplishments."

"True, but pride can be a negative when you can't admit your faults."

"If I don't have faults, there's nothing to admit," Nate said triumphantly.

Laughing, Angela threw her hands into the air. "I give up."

The waiter arrived with their dinner, topped up their wine and quietly left. Conversation ceased as they started to eat. Between bites Nate asked, "What's your favorite thing?"

"That's better." Knife and fork poised over her chicken fillet, she thought a moment. "I can't choose just one thing."

"All right, thing*s*. As in, raindrops on roses, et cetera."

"I like all those plus the scent of roses, dew on a summer morning, the sound of waves crashing on the shore, Ricky's laughter at his own silly jokes...." She ran out of ideas. "Your turn."

"Let's see... A clean run on a difficult single track, the hot tub on a starlit winter night, cold brew on a scorching summer day." He paused, thinking. "Getting a prediction right when the Department of Meteorology got it wrong—"

"Tut tut. There's that pride again."

"—kissing you."

Her eyes flashed to his. "I beg your pardon?"

He held her gaze and drew out the words. "Kissing...you."

Her fingers tightened around her fork. "We've gotten away from our original premise of pretending we're strangers."

"Does it matter? The point was to get to learn more about each other. I think we've made progress."

"I guess you're right. I've enjoyed tonight."

"Me, too." With his free hand, he reached for hers and linked fingers on top of the table.

They finished dinner then lingered over coffee on the terrace where the lush baroque sounds of the string quartet drifted up from the square. A waxing three-quarter moon rose above the steep peaks of the hotels, softening the dark blue sky with silvery light.

Angela studied Nate's profile as he relaxed and

listened to the music. Did he realize that even though she could identify his faults she still loved him? Could he love *her*, warts and all?

"Ready to go?" he asked when the music finished and the musicians began packing away their instruments. "I'll walk you to your car."

He put his arm around her shoulder as they strolled in companionable silence down the cobbled street to where she'd parked. She unlocked the Dodge then turned to Nate, reluctant to say good-night.

"Angela." His voice was soft and serious as he stroked her hair back from her temple. "All the time you were gone, I never forgot you. Not for one second."

Her heart filled. Unable to speak, she gave him a tremulous smile.

"May I kiss you?" he murmured, reaching his other hand around her waist and gently drawing her nearer.

"I'd like that very much." She raised her face to his.

As Nate's lips touched hers she melted into his arms, pliant against his framework of muscle and bone. The kiss was soft and warm as the summer breeze whispering over her bare shoulders. Their earlier kisses had been about lust and impulse. This kiss was born from desire, yes, but desire tempered by respect and genuine affection and an almost overwhelming tenderness.

Then the mood of the kiss changed. She sensed both his smoldering need and his corresponding self-control as he tried not to deepen the kiss and take more than she was ready to give.

So it was she who pushed at his closed mouth with her tongue, forcing open his lips with gentle insistence and sparking a flood of sensations that had them clinging to each other. She should stop now, but she was fast losing the will to do so. Then Nate's arms tightened around her in one convulsive hug before he released her.

"I'd better say good night," he said, his voice ragged. "But let's do this again. I'm sure there's much more to you than I found out tonight."

"I'm not going to tell you everything," she teased. "Some things you'll have to discover for yourself."

"That," he murmured, dipping his head for one last stolen kiss, "will be my pleasure. I'll see you at Kerry's tomorrow."

CHAPTER TWELVE

KERRY'S MUFFINS WERE everything Nate had promised—light, moist, bursting with juicy berries. Angela mingled while Nate talked to Kerry in a corner love seat nestled between luxurious potted palms. Seeing them laughing together didn't bother Angela a bit. Nate had assured her he and Kerry were just friends and she believed him. She wasn't as certain Kerry's feelings were platonic but she couldn't do anything about that.

Angela sipped her champagne and orange juice and turned her attention to the man at her elbow, a movie producer staying at Kerry's bed-and-breakfast while filming in Whistler. Tony was an attractive man in his late thirties with a faint English accent. She didn't have the slightest interest in him.

"You have lovely skin," Tony was saying. "Have you ever thought about acting? I might be able to get you a walk-on in my movie."

"Acting—me?" Angela laughed. "I almost singlehandedly ruined my high-school production of

Li'l Abner when I danced my way into the painted backdrop, knocking it over and pinning the two leads underneath as they waited to go on stage.''

Tony chuckled. ''So you're not a dancer. There are plenty of other roles for beautiful women like yourself.''

Even tipsy, Angela knew when she was being fed a line. But he was cute enough for her not to mind an innocent flirtation. Nate, she was gratified to see, had noticed Tony's interest in Angela and was glancing in their direction. Angela smiled and waved at him.

Tony followed the direction of her gaze. ''Friend of yours?''

''He's my husband,'' Angela said mischievously.

''Is that so? I'd watch him if I were you, darling.'' Tony topped up her drink with straight champagne. ''He's pretty cozy with our hostess.''

''They date occasionally,'' Angela replied, sipping her replenished drink. The devil was in her today. Or was it too much champagne before noon on a Sunday? She was grateful Ricky was downstairs playing video games with Tim and not witnessing his aunt's intemperate display.

Tony's eyebrows disappeared beneath the shock of hair over his forehead. ''You Canadians are more liberated than I thought.'' He touched his champagne flute to the bare skin below her collarbone and his hand brushed the tops of her breasts. "I have some movie stills upstairs in my room. Would you like to see them?"

"No, thank you…really." Angela spotted Nate getting up from the love seat and backed away from Tony's wandering hand. "If you'll excuse me, I need to ask my husband if I'll be seeing him tonight."

"If you change your mind, I'll be right here." And with that, he drifted toward the open doors leading onto the balcony where some sweet young thing was innocently taking in the view.

Angela felt a hand at her elbow and glanced around to see Nate, a scowl on his face. She giggled. "Uh-oh. Looks like we're in for stormy weather."

"That guy's a creep," Nate growled. "He didn't ask you out, did he?"

"Up to his room to look at his movie stills." She couldn't help tease him. "Jealous?"

"Yes, and I'm not embarrassed to admit it." Nate added with a leering smile, "Come to my house and I'll bore you to tears with graphs."

"Now there's an offer I can refuse."

They loaded up their plates from the buffet and took them to the kitchen where they could sit at the table instead of balancing their plates on their laps. Angela cleared a space among the bottles and dishes while Nate poured coffee from the large urn bubbling on the counter.

"I promised Ricky I'd take him to the lake this afternoon since it's so hot," Angela said, tucking in to buckwheat pancakes and vegetable frittata. "Want to come?"

"Sounds good." Nate undid the button of his breast pocket and slid out a photograph which he passed to her in silence. It was a copy of the one of them on top of the mountain.

"Oh, Nate. Thank you." She put down her knife and fork and put her arms around his neck. The future was far from being resolved but just for this moment nothing more needed to be said.

And then Nate was kissing her on the mouth, opening her lips with the firm pressure of his tongue and she could taste coffee and blueberries. He moved a hand around to cup her breast in an embrace that was intimate without being overtly sexual, restrained but with the promise of passion to come.

Footsteps sounded on the tiled floor and Angela broke free of the kiss to look over Nate's shoulder. "Hi, Kerry."

"Don't let me interrupt," Kerry said and crossed the room to deposit a stack of dirty plates near the sink.

"We're done," Nate said, and with a smile for Angela, added, "For now."

"A few people are leaving," Kerry said. "The diehards are settling in for the afternoon. What about you two?"

"We'll be off, too," Nate said.

"First we'll help clean up," Angela offered.

"Absolutely not," Kerry said, waving the suggestion away. "Myrna and Louise are staying to help while their husbands watch the football game on TV."

"Okay, but thanks for brunch," Angela said. "The food was wonderful. Maybe sometime you can show me how to make this frittata."

"Anytime. Just come over. I mean it."

"I'll go find Ricky," Nate said and glanced at Angela, eyebrows raised. "Tim?"

"Would Tim like to come swimming in the lake with us?" Angela asked Kerry, picking up on Nate's hint.

"I'm sure he would," Kerry said, adding to Nate, "They're downstairs in the rumpus room."

Nate exited, leaving Kerry and Angela gazing at one another across the room.

"So," Kerry said, smiling.

Angela returned her smile. "You know how I said Nate and I weren't involved?"

Kerry tilted her head to one side. "Yes?"

"That's changed. We're seeing each other again." No apology, no making sure Kerry didn't mind.

"I'm delighted. Truly."

Angela let out her breath. "I'm relieved you feel that way. I was afraid that in spite of what you said about you two just being friends that…well, you know."

"I've known Nate for a long time," Kerry said. "I could have fallen for him but he never quite let me in. However, he and I *are* friends. I'd like to be friends with you, too."

"That would be great." A genuine smile lifted the corners of Angela's mouth.

"And if you ever want me to take Ricky overnight," Kerry added with a wink, "just say the word."

The sounds of the boys' voices coming closer made Kerry move over to Angela. "What did you think of Tony? Is he a hottie, or what?"

"He's certainly very attractive. But I wouldn't trust him an inch."

Kerry grinned. "Oh, I know. He's the kind of guy who's here for a good time, not a long time. At the moment that happens to suit me just fine."

"Well, have fun." Angela glanced over at Nate, waiting in the doorway for her. Unlike Kerry she wanted love, home and hearth, the whole shebang.

For the first time since she'd arrived back in Whistler, she thought she just might find it.

THE NEXT MORNING Nate knocked on Angela's door with his manuscript pages bound in elastic bands and tucked under his arm. The pages were merely an excuse to see her again; they'd said good-night less than eight hours ago.

She opened the door bleary-eyed, hair uncombed and in her dressing gown, saw him and shrieked, "What are you doing here so early?"

"May I come in?" he said, stepping past her into the entrance.

"It would appear you already are," she said dryly, deliberately repeating his words from an earlier encounter back to him.

"I just have time for a coffee—" he scooped her close with his free arm "—and a kiss."

"Ack!" she exclaimed, and clamped a hand over her mouth with a muffled explanation. "Morning breath."

He nuzzled her neck instead, nipping her earlobe and sliding his hand down past her waist.

She slipped out of his arms and gave him a sleepy half smile, half frown. "What *are* you doing here?"

"I brought you what I've done so far of my book," he said, holding up the unwieldy bundle of papers. "If you meant what you said the other night about wanting to take a look."

"Sure." She tightened the belt on her dressing gown and led the way to the kitchen. Yawning, she filled the kettle at the sink, twitching back the curtains to see a faintly rosy dawn sky. She snapped awake, turning on him with an outraged glare. "The sun isn't even up!"

"I go for a training ride every day before work. I forgot you weren't a morning person."

"Morning? It's still last night," she grumbled.

He gave her a slow smile. "I could be persuaded to go back to bed."

She shook her head. "Don't even think about it."

"Sorry, not an option," he said in a low growl. "You're on my mind 24/7." It wasn't easy but he was keeping himself under control until she gave him the signal she was ready to go beyond kisses and holding hands. Their long-term future, more important than a roll in the hay, was at stake. "Maybe I should go."

"No, no." She waved him back to his seat. "I'm up now." With the kettle on, she slumped into a chair opposite him and rested her chin in her palm. "Tell me again what this race is you're training for?"

"The Gravity Fest downhill championship. It's this Wednesday."

The kettle whistled and Angela got up to make the coffee. She'd just poured the water when the phone rang. "Who on earth could be calling at this hour?" she muttered and reached for the receiver. "Hello? Stan! What a surprise. It's good to hear from you. Are you surviving that heat wave in Toronto?"

Nate's ears pricked up at the word Toronto. Who was Stan? She'd never mentioned anyone by that name. Unabashedly, he listened in on her end of the conversation, not that he had much choice, short of leaving the room.

As if aware of Nate's thoughts, she put her hand over the receiver and mouthed at him, "It's my old boss at the *Globe and Mail*."

That explained the early timing of the call; Toronto was three hours ahead of the West Coast and the workday would be just starting there. Nate didn't like it one bit. With the divorce still hanging over his head and Angela's tenure at the magazine in doubt, he was wary of anything that might pull her back East. Sure they'd been getting along great lately but he'd thought once before they were solid and look how that had turned out.

Nate got up to get the milk out of the fridge and

add it to the coffee. He stirred a cup and handed it to Angela.

She nodded her thanks and said to her caller, "She is? Congratulations! Have they set a date? So soon? You and Theresa must be going nuts trying to organize the wedding on such short notice. I'd love to come! Although I'm looking after my nephew till the end of the month. Okay, I'll see if I can manage a few days."

She was going to Toronto. Nate sipped his coffee, telling himself not to overreact. Just when he thought the conversation would wind down, she was saying, "Congratulations!" for the second time. "No one deserves that promotion more than you," she went on. There followed a long pause during which Angela listened to her caller with growing seriousness. Finally she dragged out a chair and sat down with a thump. "Oh, Stan, I don't know what to say."

Say goodbye and hang up, Nate thought, his gaze never leaving her troubled face. Clearly she was torn over whatever her ex-boss was trying to get her to do.

"I—I'll have to think about it," she said. Her eyes flashed to Nate and quickly away. "But thanks for calling and I'll see you soon. Yes, okay, slot me in. But I can't promise anything."

The click of the receiver was followed by several seconds of silence. Nate waited for her to speak.

"Stan's daughter is getting married and they want me to come to the wedding."

Nate nodded. That much he'd got. "What else?"

"He's been promoted and his old job is being advertised. He wants me to apply. He's on the selection committee."

In other words, she had a very good chance at getting it. Nate's heart sank. "Good job, is it?"

Angela smiled wanly. "One I'd be crazy to pass up."

"What are you going to do?"

"I'll go to the wedding." She took her coffee and went to stand by the sink, looking out at the mountains. Finally she turned back to him. "I agreed to be interviewed. It doesn't mean I'll accept if they offer me the position."

"Do you want me to look after Ricky again?"

"Thanks for offering, but Kerry mentioned something about Tim's father taking the boys camping on Vancouver Island for a couple of days. I'll see if I can time my trip to coincide with that."

"Okay…" There didn't seem to be anything more to say, and yet, Nate felt as though she was leaving the most important things unsaid. Like, *I'll miss you. I'll look forward to seeing you when I get back.* And *I'm not going to move across the country just when we're getting to know each other again.*

"I'll call you when I get back." Angela's smile didn't quite reach her eyes as she searched his— for what, a reason not to go? She had to come to that conclusion herself because a stubborn streak of pride gripped his tongue. He could see going to the wedding but the *interview?* The mere fact she'd agreed to do it stood in the way of them taking the next step in becoming a couple.

"See you then." Nate gripped her shoulder and kissed her cheek briefly and clumsily.

He pedaled down the road with very mixed feelings about the progress, if you could call it that, of their troubled relationship. Seemed as though they were forever going one step forward, two steps back.

ANGELA FLEW OUT of Toronto less than forty-eight hours after arriving. The interview had gone well and it was a plum job, but she felt no enthusiasm for a position she would once have jumped at. Aside from Stan's daughter's wedding, which was wonderful, everything about her trip had seemed wrong—the humidity, the traffic, even the very *flatness* of the city irritated her.

But as her return flight descended into Vancou-

ver she didn't feel the relief at coming home she'd
expected, not with Nate and her job here still up
in the air. She was at a crossroads, tantalizingly
within reach of her dreams but something was
holding her back. And that something, she decided,
was her. Until she shook loose her childhood in-
securities she wouldn't feel worthy of Nate, much
less capable of sustaining a marriage.

Ricky was still away camping with Tim and his
dad when Angela drove into Whistler late on Saturday evening. She thought about calling Nate but
didn't want to see him while she was in this confused state. They'd been going so well until her
vulnerability and his pride had thrown up barriers
neither could bring themselves to penetrate. As
he'd said, if they fell in love again, they had so
much more to lose.

Sunday morning she was still restless. Not
knowing what else to do she got in the station
wagon and started driving north on Highway 99 to
Pemberton.

IN DEFERENCE TO THE WEEKEND, Nate had slept in;
the sun was over the mountains before he got on
his bike and headed to the highway for his training
ride. The fine weather was holding and below his
churning legs the smooth black pavement slipped
away. He ignored the roar of blood in his ears and

the burn of lactic acid in his muscles and simply concentrated on his breathing. Out for three beats, in for two. Out for three, in for two. And so on until the pumping of the pedals and the movement of air in and out of his lungs combined to create a hypnotic state in which he skated up hills and sped down, piling mile upon mile on his odometer. Deep in the rhythm of the ride he felt no pain, only the release of endorphins that turned endurance into sweat-drenched ecstasy.

He was passing the north end of Green Lake, slowing to drink from his water bottle, when he noticed his father's truck parked in front of a log-home-construction site and decided to pull in. He hadn't talked to his dad since his mother's birthday party and the truth was, he could use a sounding board about his relationship with Angela.

The air was split by the heavy thud of logs sliding into place and scented with the tangy resin of yellow cedar as a team of carpenters built up the walls of the log home, one thick row at a time. Nate picked his way through the mud and the off-cuts to where Jim was poring over a set of building plans.

"Hey, Dad," Nate said and Jim glanced around. "How's it going?"

"Not bad. Looking for a job? I can always use a good carpenter."

''Thanks, but no thanks. I just stopped to say hello.''

''A long way to ride to say hello.'' Jim's sharp gaze searched Nate's face. ''Something on your mind?''

''As a matter of fact—''

Just then another truck rolled onto the construction site. ''That'll be the plumber,'' Jim said. ''Can you hang on while I talk to this guy for a second? He's on double time.''

''Don't worry. I can see you don't have time right now for a father-son chat. I'll stop by the house later. It's nothing urgent, just wanted your advice on Angela.''

''In a nutshell?'' Jim said, eyes twinkling. ''Ride real hard and you might catch her.''

Nate frowned. ''What do you mean? She's still in Toronto.''

Jim started walking over to the plumber, Nate at his side. ''I'm positive that was her I saw in Janice's old green Dodge. I was slowing down to turn in here when she came up behind. She tooted her horn and waved as she went past.''

Nate got on his bike and pedaled hard.

Twenty minutes later he spun through the roundabout at the entrance to Pemberton. Reaching for his water bottle, he took a long draft then continued up the main street past the primary school and the Pemberton Hotel. There was no sign of Angela or the green Dodge though he rode up and down the few short streets of the town center.

Heading out the other side of town he cruised down a country road through acres of flat pastureland bordered by purple mountains rising steeply from the Lillouette River valley. Cows, horses and even alpacas grazed in bucolic idyll.

He presumed he'd missed her and was about to go back to the highway when on impulse he turned down the narrow road that led to the riverside trailer park where Angela had lived as a girl.

Thick stands of fir and spruce trees shaded the gravel lane that looped through the trailer park. The shabby old single wide she'd grown up in was long gone. Most of the mobile homes remaining were well cared for, with flowers in barrels outside the door and patches of grass between the lanes where kids rode their bikes. A woman with a baby on her hip and a toddler clinging to her legs stood in an open doorway and stared as he rode past.

Nate took the rutted track down to the river. He saw the Dodge first, parked only yards from the broad rushing stream. Angela, in a sleeveless blouse and short denim skirt, was sitting on a huge granite boulder. With the sound of the moving water and the crows cawing overhead, she hadn't noticed his arrival. She had a stick in her hand and was tracing it over the veins in the rock, her gaze turned inward.

Nate dismounted, took off his helmet and leather gloves and walked toward her, the light breeze cooling his drying sweat. Only when his bike shoes crunched on the pebbles did she become aware of his presence.

"What are you doing here?" she asked, surprised. Dried tear tracks snaked down her cheeks.

"I was on a training ride. Dad said he saw you heading in this direction." He climbed onto the boulder and sat next to her. "Want to talk about it?"

She shrugged and remained silent.

"How was Toronto?"

"Hot, crowded, flat. The wedding was lovely."

"And the interview?"

"It went well." She glanced at him, her expression unreadable. "I'll probably be offered the job."

Nate waited. After another long pause, he asked, "Are you going to tell me whether you'll take it or do I have to ask?"

She smiled, a sad smile. "I don't *want* to. I may have to."

Nate gazed out over the river. No one *had* to do anything they didn't want to do. He dropped the subject for the moment. "This place must bring back old memories."

Angela began to tap the boulder with her stick in an agitated manner. "The thing about memories is," she said in a strained voice, "you can't ever really escape them."

"What do you mean?"

A bald eagle swooped low over the water, scanning for fish. She turned to Nate and he was shocked to see her eyes flooded with fresh tears.

"Do you recall at the restaurant when I was telling you about my seventh birthday?" she said. He nodded. "I hid it, but in fact I was very distressed."

"You were a child deprived of a much-anticipated treat," he murmured even though that sounded overblown to him. Clearly she'd omitted something important from her account of the event. He took her hand. It felt cold and small inside his.

She shook her bowed head, her bright hair falling around her face. "That wasn't it. A few days before my birthday my father walked out on my mom."

He chafed her hand, trying to bring some warmth back into it. "I'm so sorry, Ange. That must have been awful for your mom and traumatic for you and Janice."

Angela brushed the tears from her flushed

cheeks and said bitterly, "We watched the whole thing, Janice and I, from our bedroom door. Mom was sobbing and clinging to him, literally hanging on to his jacket. As he was going out the door, she fell on her knees, saying over and over, 'I love you, I love you, I love you.'" Each time Angela said the word "love" she snapped another piece off the stick.

Nate's heart constricted with pain for her. "What did your father do?"

"He snarled and shook her off like...a *dog*. It was the most humiliating scene I've ever witnessed. We never saw him again and good riddance. I don't think he was even our father." Angela threw away the pieces of stick and released a long deep sigh as she lifted soul-weary eyes that had no tears left to shed. "I was just a kid but I was so ashamed for her. I vowed I would never be that poor, or that dependent on a man."

"I knew your home life was bleak but I had no idea it was that bad," Nate said. "No wonder your mother was too upset to celebrate even something as simple as your birthday."

"No, it's worse than that." Angela's voice was taut with misery. "That's when she started drinking. She went on a bender and by the time my birthday came around she was incapable of fixing dinner much less organizing a birthday party. From that time on I was more or less in charge at home, until she met a trucker and moved to Prince George when I was seventeen. We didn't hear from her again until the news came that she died of liver disease. I felt like I never really had a mother.''

Nate swore helplessly as anger surged through him toward the adults who'd failed her. Then he gathered her in his arms and the anger was followed by a wave of tenderness for that outwardly tough but inwardly fragile little girl who'd learned to fend not only for herself but also for her mother and sister.

Angela could break, just like anyone else.

She clung to him now, her face buried in his chest, her sobs mingling with the soughing of the wind in the pines and the low rush of water over stones. Nate held her and rocked her as he would a child, murmuring semicoherent words of comfort and love.

At last she recovered enough to pull back and catch her breath. ''I'm sorry, Nate. You must think I'm a great big crybaby.''

''You earned that, Ange.'' Pushing her hair out of her face, he dotted kisses on her reddened eyes, her temple and down her cheeks.

She pressed her hands against his damp shirt. ''I've soaked you with tears.''

Nate chuckled. ''Relax. Most of that's sweat.

I've been cycling for hours.'' He searched her eyes and found some sadness but also a new serenity. ''Are you okay?''

Her blue eyes shimmering, she nodded. ''Thanks for being here. Besides Janice, no one knows me like you do.''

''I'm your husband, after all.''

Inside the circle of his arms, Angela lowered her gaze and went very still. He'd dropped a clanger. But *damn* he was tired of playing this game.

''I don't—'' he began.

''I didn't—'' she started to say.

''—want a divorce.''

''—file.''

They'd both spoken at once and for a moment he stared at her and she stared back, each uncertain of what they'd heard.

''You didn't file for divorce?'' he asked.

She nodded. ''And you're happy about that?''

''Yes. *Yes!*'' He hugged her hard, his chest expanding till it almost hurt. Smiling into her eyes, he wiped tears from her cheeks then his mouth found hers in a warm and lingering kiss.

His close embrace pressed their bodies together as he lay down with her on the sun-warmed rock.

She murmured huskily, ''Nate, I want you.''

He wished he could take her right there on the

riverbank but their first lovemaking in ten years had to be special. He knew just the place to go.

"Drive home," he whispered. "Put on sturdy shoes. I'll pick you up as soon as I can get back."

CHAPTER THIRTEEN

AN HOUR LATER ANGELA heard Nate's Jeep Cherokee pull into the driveway. She laced on her trainers and ran outside to climb into the passenger side. "Where are we going?"

He'd showered and changed into hiking shorts and a loose cotton shirt. His arms and legs were tanned and well muscled. "You'll find out soon enough."

He drove into the Village and parked in one of the day lots then steered her toward the Whistler Mountain gondola. Seeing his backpack with the rolled-up blanket tied to the top she felt a shiver of anticipation. They were going up the mountain to the secluded knoll where they'd shared their first kiss and where he'd proposed to her.

They rode the gondola as far as it went then walked over to the quad chairlift that would take them to the very peak. Angela stood beside Nate on the marker line and the quadchair scooped them up with a sudden rocking lurch. They swung gently a few times then settled down as the chair lifted above the ground, steadily gaining altitude until they were level with the tips of the fir trees that lined either side of the ski run below.

The brilliant blue sky, the dazzling white glacier-topped peaks, Nate's arm around her shoulders... It was one of those rare moments of pure happiness. Then he brought his mouth down to hers. Warm lips, cool air. Anchored to Nate's heat and solid muscle Angela poured her heart and soul into a long glorious kiss.

Finally they broke off, grinning idiotically at each other. Angela's eye caught a movement on a rocky outcropping below.

"Look at the marmots." She pointed to a dozen or so of the large gopherlike creatures sunning themselves.

Suddenly the marmots stood erect on their hind legs at the sound of an animal or a hiker crashing through the woods bordering the ski run.

"Listen!" Nate said. "You can hear them whistling to alert each other to danger. You know, of course—"

"That's how Whistler got its name." Angela elbowed him in the ribs. "I'm a local, remember?"

"Could have fooled me, these past ten years."

"Are you going to keep throwing that in my face?"

"You're right," he said. "It's time we got past all that. Once a local, always a local."

The air was noticeably cooler when they got off the chairlift a short time later but still warm in the sun. Nate hoisted his pack on his back. The trail they followed traversed an alpine meadow blooming with wildflowers whose colorful heads nodded in the breeze.

Past the meadow the trail dropped in elevation to enter the forest, dwindled to little more than a deer track then petered out altogether. Nate led the way through thick stands of conifers guided only by his sense of direction. After a while they started climbing again. The trees thinned and became interspersed with huge rocky outcroppings which they scrambled over or around.

Just when Angela was beginning to think Nate's instincts had failed him for once and they were completely lost, they emerged onto a grassy knoll clinging to the rocky mountainside.

The small patch of lush grass was dotted with wildflowers and lit by the westering sun—a miniature Shangri-la. Ahead of them and on all sides, peak after peak of dazzling white glaciers atop mountains cloaked in vast forests seemed to stretch into infinity.

Angela caught her breath, staring in awe at the

grandeur of her surroundings. They might have been the only two people on the planet.

Nate spread the blanket on the grass and gestured to her to sit down. ''There you go. Front-row seats to the most spectacular show on earth.''

He unpacked a simple picnic—white wine, brie cheese, ripe tomatoes and fresh French bread. A cutting board and knife was pulled from his backpack, and wrapped in tea towels, two crystal goblets. Angela held the heavy glasses steady while Nate poured. The crystal glasses were another wedding present; using them seemed not only fitting but symbolic.

Setting the bottle to one side, he clinked his glass with hers. ''To us.''

''To us,'' she echoed and sipped her wine. Fruity and dry, the chill liquid warmed her blood. Nate got out his Swiss Army knife and cut off chunks of bread and cheese and sliced the tomato. Angela watched his fingers and half in memory, half in fantasy, pictured those hands moving over her body. They ate and drank, talking of trivialities while their eyes spoke of more important matters.

Gradually the food and conversation ran out. Angela studied Nate's profile as he gazed over the valley—the bump in his nose, the outdoorsman's squint, his full lower lip. ''Have you ever brought anyone else here?''

His eyes met hers and he shook his head.

A look, an unspoken thought, passed between them. Without another word, they packed away the remains of the food, brushed the crumbs off the blanket and moved closer together. Lightly kissing her lips, her neck, her collarbone, Nate eased her down on the blanket until they were lying face-to-face, barely touching. Her blood singing with wine and happiness, Angela looked into his eyes, drinking in every beloved detail. His gaze caressed her face with equal intensity until the air between them seemed to catch fire with the force of their mutual longing.

As if unable to resist any longer, he reached up to touch her face, tracing the curve of her cheek with his fingertips, brushing a thumb across her bottom lip. ''I've been walking around half-alive without you.''

Angela slid a hand inside the open collar of his buttoned shirt; his heated skin and firm muscle sent tingling sensations through her palm and fingertips. ''I fooled myself into thinking that what I had in Toronto was a life.''

His hand curled around her nape, drawing her to him. Her fingers moved up his shoulders to his neck and into his hair, thick and soft as a skein of silk. Patches of sunlight warmed her back and her thigh. His hand moved down, covering her breast and she moaned and edged closer still, pressing her hips against his. The rigid lines of his back gave evidence of the battle between the force of his desire and the power of his control.

Breaking the kiss, he worked open the row of tiny buttons down the front of her top, gazing at her gradually revealed breasts with eyes hot and dark. "Next time wear something else," he muttered. "Like a towel."

He pushed aside the flimsy fabric and her breasts swelled above the low curve of her bra. With a groan he lowered his head and pulled aside white lace to suck her nipple into his mouth.

Her own control began to dwindle fast. The pulling sensation in first one breast then the other aroused a throbbing ache between her legs that rendered her paralyzed with need. With his mouth and tongue taking care of her nipples, his hand slid up under her skirt, bunching the fabric high on her thighs.

She tugged blindly at his shirt, desperate to feel his skin against hers. "This *has* to go," she said. *"Now."*

"Hang on." He rose above her to strip off his shirt and shorts, taking something from his pocket before he tossed his clothes aside. She lay on her back staring up at him silhouetted against the sky. His hard sculpted body was, quite simply, breathtaking. And with his dark tousled hair falling over his forehead he looked sexy and endearing at the same time.

She raised her arms to draw him down. He fell to his hands and knees over her, bending his head to kiss while she smoothed her hands over his chest and sides. She traced the ridges of scars: some old, some new. They pained her as if she'd received the injuries herself. She wished briefly, helplessly, that she'd told him about the miscarriage before they'd become intimate again. If they were to live together and be husband and wife in more than just name they should have no secrets between them.

But at the moment making love was all she could think of. Nate was completely, gloriously naked; she was still partially clothed. The contrast was erotic. "Nate," she moaned. "Make love to me."

At her provocative words and husky voice Nate's blood surged and his erection grew hotter, harder, higher. The years and weeks of waiting and wanting coalesced into an aching driving need. Angela, with her blouse open and falling off her shoulders and her skirt around her waist exposing shapely tanned legs below white-lace panties, had the look of a lustful virgin, sexy and pure, alluring in her innocence, irresistible in her desire. She was his wife, she was a stranger. She was the woman he'd held only in his dreams for too many years.

Her breasts rose and fell with each shortened breath. Her irises had darkened to dusky blue and the black pupils reached deep into his, as though she was looking into his dreams, or maybe seeing her own reflected in his eyes.

He lowered himself half on top of her, kissing her lightly and fondling her, taking a torturous pleasure in holding back. Her restless fingers roamed his chest and rigid back, touching and stroking as she reacquainted herself with him. He pulled back a little, wanting to see her as much as touch and kiss her. Moving lower, he kissed the graze on her knee then pressed kisses on his way up her leg, a hand splayed across her thigh, turning it out so he could access the soft inner skin. Her back arched when he reached the mound at the apex of her legs. Slipping down her panties, he tasted her, once, twice, until she writhed and tugged on his hair, drawing him up to her.

He hunted in the folds of the blankets for the condom and put it on. Her eyebrows rose. Unabashed, he said, ''Would you rather I come unprepared?''

She smiled at his double entendre, and shook her head.

He pushed into her, felt her body tighten around

him and draw him farther in. Her mouth found his, blindly, and they moved in rhythm, slow at first, then faster and faster. Angela had come home. He'd won her back. It was as simple and primal, as complex and wondrous, as that.

And when they came, they came together, their mingled cries of pleasure floating over the vast silence of the valley, echoing faintly off the mountains to sound again in their ears.

Angela lay satiated and deeply content, blanketed by Nate's warm weight, savoring the musky scent of his body. The slick layer of perspiration covering his skin gradually cooled and the thud of his heart slowed while she listened to his lengthening breaths. His face was buried in her neck and when she stirred at last, he rolled off her, pulling her with him so they lay on their sides, face-to-face, as they'd begun.

"It's been a long time, Mrs. Wilde."

"I hope it won't be ten years till the next time."

"The way I feel, it'll be ten minutes."

Suddenly they both smiled, mouths curving wide and high. Angela only wished she'd sought a second chance with Nate sooner. She would make him happy if it took every ounce of her strength and courage.

Rising on one elbow she said, "Did you bring anything nonalcoholic to drink? I'm parched."

Nate got up and went to his backpack, returning with a bottle of springwater.

"Thanks." She drank thirstily.

He lay on his side, head propped on his hand. "You've been in Whistler almost four weeks. Janice and Bob will be back soon."

"Saturday," she said, offering him the bottle. "Ricky and I will drive to Vancouver to pick them up at the airport."

Angela wondered what Nate was thinking. Were they on the same wavelength about the future? She loved him but would he ask her to come back? Did she have the courage to broach the subject? Did she have the *right* until she confessed all that happened on that freezing night in late January ten years ago?

Watching his face closely for his reaction, she said, "I've been thinking I might move back to Whistler."

The brightening flicker in his face *wasn't* her imagination. "That's the best news I've heard all day."

"I would keep my apartment," she said. "For a while anyway, until I see how much time I need to spend there."

"An apartment in the city would be handy," Nate replied. "Maybe you wouldn't mind if I used it when I visit my Vancouver bike store. I'd contribute to the rent, of course.''

''Sure. No problem.'' Sharing accommodation was surely the first step to living together, and to being married in more than name only. She wanted fervently for them to be husband and wife again but she was afraid to suggest it outright. If he said no after what they'd just shared she didn't think she could bear it.

Nate picked at minute crumbs in the folds of the blanket. ''You're welcome to stay with me while you're in Whistler.''

''Thanks.'' She hoped she sounded as nonchalant as he did even though her breath was tight in her chest. ''Janice doesn't have an extra bedroom and I can't afford two places—''

She broke off, aware she'd just revealed that if she couldn't afford two places and couldn't stay with Janice, then a return to Whistler meant she'd been counting on living with Nate from the first.

Nate regarded her with indulgent humor. ''Come here, you little schemer,'' he said, pulling her into his arms. ''I wouldn't let you live anywhere but with me.''

His warm and lingering kiss left her in no doubt of his sincerity but Angela's conscience was hurting. Part of her brain told her to leave well enough alone; they were back together and that was all that mattered. Another part of her insisted she would never feel right unless he knew the worst and had forgiven her.

"Nate?" Reluctantly she drew back from him. "There's something I need to tell you."

"Women," he said with tender exasperation. "Talk, talk, talk." Smoothing a strand of hair behind her ear, he added, "Okay, what is it?"

Angela's gaze flickered between his serious dark eyes and his full bottom lip. She swallowed and took a deep breath, telling herself he would understand. He had to. The alternative—losing him a second time, possibly forever—was unthinkable.

Meeting his eyes squarely, she forced herself to say the words. "That night I left I was—"

A shaft of the setting sun struck her full in the face and she raised a hand to shield her eyes. She sat up, alarmed. It was much later than she'd realized.

"What were you saying?" Nate asked, lazily stroking her arm.

"I'll tell you after. We'd better go. It'll be dark soon and we need to find our way back to the chairlift." The light was failing. She *wasn't* just stalling—although there might have been an element of that in her hurry to be gone.

Quickly they dressed and gathered up their things. Nate rolled the blanket and lashed it to the top of his pack. When they were ready Angela headed out immediately. She'd walked to the edge of the woods before she noticed Nate had lingered to watch the rays of rosy sunlight illuminating the steep forested slope of neighboring Blackcomb Mountain. Then like a light switching off, the sun dropped behind the mountains and the forest turned to shades of dusky gray.

"Come on." She strode back to tug on his arm. She'd only brought a light sweater and they had at least a half hour walk back to the chairlift through pathless woods much darker than where they now stood. "I don't want to get caught on the mountain. It might be summer but we're not prepared for spending a night out here."

He reached for her hand with an unconcerned smile. "Don't worry. I'll get you back to the chairlift. But if we did have to spend the night it'd be a story to tell our grandchildren."

At the mention of future generations, she glanced away.

"You do *want* to have children, don't you? Ange?"

"I want a dozen little rug rats. What do you think?"

As his searching gaze met her defiant stare, his

face fell. "You've got that flippant tone again," he said dully. "I think you're hiding something."

NATE WAITED FOR ANGELA to tell him what was on her mind but she kept her eyes fixed on the ground, stubbornly repeating, "We've got to get back."

One glance at the deepening gloom in the forest ahead of them and he slung his backpack on his back. "You're right. We'll talk later."

At the edge of the knoll, Nate paused to take his bearings then plunged into the woods, looking not down or sideways but straight ahead in the direction he wanted to go. They walked some distance in silence while the night descended on the forest. Bushes scratched at their legs, unseen roots made them stumble. Nate breathed a sigh of relief when at last the narrow deer trail materialized out of the twilight.

From there it was relatively easy to find their way back to the chairlift station. Floodlights lining the ski run came on as they rode the quadchair down, making the surrounding dusk seem even darker. Below, the lights of Whistler glowed brightly as the resort's restaurants and pubs came to life. Beside him, Angela hugged her arms about herself, shivering in the cool night air.

Nate pulled her close and rubbed her arms in an attempt to warm her. "What were you going to say up on the mountain?"

She glanced at him quickly, and away. "That night I left..."

The past again. "I thought we had that out. We were both young and headstrong. We didn't communicate. Let's put it behind us."

"There's something you don't know about that time."

An undercurrent in her voice gave him a bad feeling, but he said calmly, "Just tell me. You can trust me."

Angela spoke quickly as if anxious to get it all out before she lost her nerve. "I—I was pregnant."

"Pregnant!" He felt the blood drain from his face.

"About eight weeks is my best guess." She stared out into the dark. "I should have told you..."

Chilled by her startling admission, Nate withdrew his arm, needing what little warmth it imparted for himself. Her sudden flight, her refusal to come home, her long absence—all took on new significance. In a strained voice, he asked, "Do we have a child somewhere?"

"What? No! I miscarried that same night. I don't know if it was the trauma of our fight and running away, or whether the accident had something to do with it—"

"Accident! You never told me about any accident. Were you hurt?"

"Nothing you could see except a small cut on my hand when I was thrown out of my seat. It was snowing and the streets were icy. I was on the bus and we were coming down that long hill in North Vancouver leading off the Upper Levels highway to Marine Drive when the brakes locked. The bus skidded off the road and into a telephone pole. We couldn't have been going more than twenty miles an hour. The front end was crumpled—"

"Forget the bus. What about you?"

"I was okay. Or so I thought." She shivered at the memory of that awful night—the bitter wind off the mountains, the driving snow, the icy sidewalks. "I got out of the bus and started walking."

"You should have stayed with the bus. Someone would have come—an ambulance or the police."

"I wasn't injured, although in hindsight I suppose I was in shock. Anyway, I set off. It was dark and very cold."

Leaning into the corner of the chairlift, Nate twisted in his seat to stare, anger and compassion warring in his heart. "Why the hell would you go all the way to Vancouver during a snowstorm?"

"I wanted to get as far away from you as possible."

After their lovemaking it was a brutal thing to say. Something inside him hardened. "Go on."

"There's not much more to tell. I slipped on the sidewalk and crashed down on my tailbone. The next thing I knew, blood was pouring down my leg. I was dazed. I thought at first I'd injured myself in the accident and not realized it. Then I felt the cramping pains in my womb and I knew. I got to a gas station and the attendant called an ambulance to take me to the hospital."

Compassion won out and he wrapped her in his arms. She melted against him, curling in to his chest. "What an ordeal. You should never have gone out on such a night. And our baby."

"I'm so sorry, Nate." Her voice, thick with emotion, was muffled against his chest. "I know how badly you wanted a child."

"Shh, it's okay," he said, massaging the back of her neck with long gentle strokes. "You didn't know."

She went still in his arms, even the sound of her breathing stopped. Nate's fingers ceased their caress.

"You *didn't* know you were pregnant, did you? *Ange?*" When after a long moment, she didn't answer, he said, his voice dull. "Let me rephrase that—how *long* had you known?"

"Two weeks."

Angela's whole being felt weighed down with sadness and guilt as she sensed him retreating emotionally. He removed his arms from around her again. She felt alone on the chairlift, freeze-dried by the wind off the glaciers, shriveled and so very cold.

"Nate?" She reached a hand out to touch his arm. He brushed it off and she cringed.

"You knew you were pregnant for two weeks and you didn't tell me?" His voice was as frigid as his eyes. "You risked our baby and ran out into a storm."

She tried reaching out to him again. As tall and broad shouldered as he was, he seemed to shrink to avoid her touch. Stung, she went on the attack. *"You let me go!* I put on my boots and coat. I packed an overnight bag and took money from the sugar canister. You watched me do all that and you didn't try to stop me. You said you assumed I went to Janice's. Why didn't you call and make sure?"

"How do you know I didn't?"

"Because I asked her, of course. Then I found out you were at the pub, drinking with your biking buddies."

"I was pissed off. The next morning when I called, why didn't she tell me you were in the hospital?"

"I told her not to, I was so mad at you." She

sucked in a deep breath. "Besides, then I would have had to tell you about the miscarriage and you would have blamed me." She paused. "I blamed myself."

"Dammit, Angela. I was your husband. You should have turned to *me,* not your sister."

Angela didn't answer. In her admittedly limited experience husbands couldn't be relied upon. And suddenly she realized she'd left Nate before he could leave her.

"I never wanted any of it to happen," she said miserably.

"Back then, when were you planning on telling me about the baby?" he demanded. Then dawning horror pervaded his voice. "Or were you planning to get rid of it?"

"No." Her gaze flashed to his, insisting he believe her. "I wouldn't have done that."

The final descent approached and the chairlift seemed to speed up before jerking to a halt. The attendant pulled back the bar and they were disgorged onto land. Angela stumbled out of the way of the chairlift.

They walked to the gondola in silence then boarded with nine or ten others making the trip the rest of the way down the mountain. Angela turned away from Nate to stare out the window. She could hardly blame him for being upset but his reaction was worse than she'd imagined. Trapped side by side in a close-packed gondola she could feel his arm pressing into her side, his thigh pushed up against her hip, but there was no warmth, only an emotional distance as wide as the valley.

Not until they were walking through the deserted parking lot toward his vehicle did he speak again.

"You're not a teenager now, Angela. You've had weeks to tell me and you spent it playing stupid games."

"Oh, and you didn't play games with me?"

"I didn't have a secret. Stop hiding behind that smart mouth of yours and grow up!" He turned away from her to unlock the car.

She stared at the rigid set of his retreating shoulders and felt her world drop into the abyss. "Nate—"

She broke off, cringing at the pleading note in her voice. What was she going to say? *I love you.* He didn't want to hear that. And she couldn't bear it if she told him and he rejected her.

Nate didn't speak another word to her on the drive home and Angela sank further into depression. What was happening between them? Was it over? She was afraid to ask.

Nate pulled into her driveway but didn't cut the engine. The streetlights illuminated the hard planes of his face as he twisted on the bench seat to face her. "Do you want me to pick up Ricky from Tim's house?"

"They're still away camping." She could have cried remembering her hopes and plans for tonight. Instead of cuddling up to Nate, she would be sleeping alone.

Something flickered in his eyes and for a moment she thought he would say something to bring them back together. Then his expression turned inward again, shutting her out. He turned and stared straight ahead, his thumbs beating a tattoo on the steering wheel while he waited for her to go.

Angela opened the car door, reluctant to leave but with no reason to linger. "When will I see you?"

"I don't know." His voice was thin and hard, leaving her little room for hope and no cause for reassurance.

Suddenly she was angry. "How can you act so coldly after making love to me?"

His face changed, became weary, and he leaned one forearm on the wheel as he twisted in his seat to look at her. "I'm in shock. I need time to process this."

"And what am I supposed to do in the meantime?"

"Get on with your life. Isn't that what you're

always talking about?'' He let out a deep, irritated sigh. ''Leave it for now, Ange. Just leave it.''

She couldn't just leave it. She hated parting without making up. Tonight felt too much like that other night, ten years ago. ''You can't just stop talking when *you've* had enough.''

He threw her a cynical glance. ''Watch me.''

''Dammit! How are we supposed to work anything out?''

''I'm tired. I was up at dawn and cycled sixty miles. I don't want to talk.''

''What about tomorrow?''

''I'm training in the morning and riding the course all afternoon. The race is the day after that.''

''Well, well, just like old times. You have fun with your bike. I hope it keeps you warm at night.'' Knowing she was being childish but unable to help herself, she got out, slammed the door and marched up the path to the front door.

CHAPTER FOURTEEN

IF HE AND ANGELA hadn't fought ten years ago, would he have a child today? The thought haunted Nate. He opened the glass-fronted cabinet next to his trophy case that housed his collection of favorite Matchbox cars. They'd been his as a kid and he'd saved them for his own kids to play with. He took them out and lined them up on the workbench: the black Corvette, the two-tone '57 Chevy, the shiny red Ford pickup. Marc reckoned he was sentimental but Nate didn't care. He liked the idea of passing on something special to his children.

He felt betrayed by Angela, and worse, not trusted.

Thinking back to that time, he tried to make sense of her actions. She'd been pregnant and unprepared to have children. He'd unwittingly pressured her to start a family. They'd argued. She'd run away. As galling as it was to his pride the only interpretation he could put on her flight was that she left because she was carrying his baby.

A man didn't throw that off easily. She couldn't have truly loved him. Did she love him now?

He could understand Angela keeping her pregnancy and miscarriage a secret from him during their long years of separation but in the past weeks she'd had numerous opportunities to mention the small matter of a baby she'd lost. If they split up this time, he knew it would be forever.

Gripping the Corvette so tightly the fins dug into his palm, he closed his eyes and grieved for the baby he'd lost and the wife he couldn't keep.

ANGELA'S ANGRY BRAVADO lasted until she heard Nate's truck drive away. Then despair overtook her, black and numbing, howling through her like a dark force. For a long time she lay curled in a tight fetal ball on the bed, unable to think or even to cry, so paralyzing was her grief. Sometime in the middle of the night she got up, stripped off her clothes and got into the shower. But her nakedness reminded her first of making love with Nate, then of her vulnerability. Racked with the pain of loss she crouched in a corner of the tiled shower. The scalding water poured over her upturned face and mingled with her salty tears.

The next morning she awoke with a dull headache and a leaden heart. All day she waited for Nate to call and make up. A thousand times she thought about calling him, and a thousand times she told herself to leave him alone. He'd gone into his metaphorical cave and wasn't coming out until he'd sorted things out in his mind.

He didn't call. *Too busy training to make time for her.* That had hurt ten years ago and it hurt even worse now. Seeing the advertising banners for the bike race up around Whistler only rubbed salt in her wounds. In the evening she sat and knitted his sweater and wondered why she bothered. He knew how miserable she was; why couldn't he take a few minutes to reassure her all was not lost?

He must not love her after all.

Don't be an idiot, a voice inside ordered. *You've had ten years to get used to the fact that you lost a child; he just found out and needs time to absorb it.*

All the rationality in the world didn't seem to help; she *needed* his reassurance. If that made her immature and childish, then that's who she was.

By the following morning she was disgusted with herself. She still longed for Nate to call but she had to acknowledge that to a large extent she'd created her own situation; hard as it was, she'd just have to tough it out.

Then the phone rang.

Angela threw back the covers and sprang to her feet. She wrapped her dressing gown around her and hurried to the kitchen, grabbing the receiver on the fifth ring.

"Hello, Nate?" she said, breathlessly.

"Angie? It's Janice. Listen, I'm calling from the airport in Rome. We're flying home. The plane gets in tomorrow morning."

"But...I wasn't expecting you back till the end of the week."

"We're returning early. Bob was taking a photo of me in front of the Trinità del Monti and he kept backing up until finally he fell down the Spanish Steps."

"Oh my God! Poor Bob. Is he all right?"

"Only a fractured leg. Luckily for him, a German tourist coming up the steps broke his fall."

"What time do you get in? I'll pick you up from the airport."

"Our flight lands at eight a.m. Wednesday. I'm sorry it's such short notice."

"No problem." Wednesday morning was Nate's bike race but the odds were high he wouldn't want her there anyway. "Ricky and I'll drive down this afternoon and stay at my apartment in Vancouver."

"I hope we're not spoiling a hot date with your ex."

"No, I managed to do that all by myself."

"What do you mean?"

Angela sighed. "We were so close to getting back together and I went and spoiled it all by telling him about the miscarriage. He didn't take it well. Part of me wants to get on a bus and leave, just as I did ten years ago."

"Don't worry, Ange. He'll come around."

"I don't know. He's pretty angry. But I'd better let you go—this is costing you a fortune. See you soon."

Angela packed her bags and spent the morning cleaning the house in preparation for Janice and Bob's return. She kept waiting for the phone to ring again and when she went to the market to stock up on milk and bread she rushed for the answering machine the moment she walked through the door. Still no call from Nate.

She decided to phone him. Her stomach full of knots, she dialed the number of his store and waited through five rings before Rachel's breathless voice came on only to say, "Cycle Sports. Hold please."

Before Angela could identify herself she had techno music filling her ears with its staccato beat. A few minutes later, Rachel was back. "May I help you?"

"It's Angela," she said quickly. "Could I speak to Nate?"

"Just a sec."

Angela paced from the kitchen to the living room and back, listening to the background buzz of voices and noises coming over the line from the store.

Finally someone picked up the phone but it was Rachel again. "Hello, Angela? I'm sorry. Nate can't talk right now. We're going crazy in here with the Gravity Fest on all week. Do you want to leave a message?"

He couldn't talk to her, or wouldn't? "No message. I...I'll try another time." She put down the phone.

"When are we going to Vancouver?" Ricky asked, breaking into her thoughts. His overnight bag was packed and standing at the front door.

"Right after lunch." She hurriedly made a sandwich and placed it in front of him. She'd planned on driving down later in the afternoon but suddenly she couldn't bear to wait by the phone another minute.

She ate quickly then got her suitcase from the bedroom, pausing on the threshold for a quick survey to ensure she hadn't forgotten anything. She'd stripped the bed and put on clean sheets, vacuumed and cleaned the bathroom.... All was ready for Janice and Bob's return.

With her visit cut short and her future with Nate

up in the air, she didn't know when, if ever, she would come back to Whistler. Swallowing a lump in her throat she shut the door behind her.

NATE PUT IN ANOTHER LONG DAY, working and training, avoiding the time when he had to go home to an empty house. Living alone had never bothered him until he'd started dreaming of Angela sharing the place with him.

Without quite realizing where he was going, he found himself driving down her street, slowing as he approached the small single-story house. He frowned. No lights were on and her car wasn't in the driveway.

Where was she? Besides himself, Kerry and his family, he wasn't aware that she'd renewed acquaintance with anyone in Whistler. He drove by Kerry's house a couple of blocks away but Angela's car wasn't there so he kept going to Aidan's house. His mother's car was parked out front.

Knocking, he entered. "Aidan? Mom? It's me, Nate."

"In the living room," Leone called. She was seated on the couch reading Emily a bedtime story but paused when he came in.

"Aidan on a date?" Nate asked, dropping to an adjacent chair.

Leone lifted her gaze from the book with a

motherly sigh. "Wouldn't that be nice? But no, he's bringing in a hiker who broke his leg on the mountain." She glanced at the gilt clock on the mantelpiece. "I expect he'll be back shortly. Let me just finish reading to Emily."

Nate listened with half an ear to *Winnie the Pooh* and looked about the room from the Austrian lace curtains to the dainty bone-china figurines on the mantel piece. Aidan really needed to update his decor. This stuff was Charmaine all over but not his brother's taste.

Restless, he got up and paced across to the study. This room, with its modern handcrafted furniture and moody landscape paintings, was the only one that showed signs of Aidan's touch. Tapping his fingers on the doorjamb, Nate wondered, as he often did, what his brother and Charmaine had had in common. Best keep those thoughts to himself, as he'd always done. Aidan didn't like talking about his relationship with his late wife, not even to his family.

Nate spun around at the sound of the front door opening. Aidan came in, looking exhausted. His eyes brightened when he spied his daughter, who bounded off the couch and ran over for a hug.

"Daddy!" she squealed, kicking her pajama-clad legs as he scooped her into his arms.

At least Aidan had Emily. Seeing them together,

his dark head bent toward her curly blond one, Nate envied his brother. The sharp ache he felt at the thought of the child he would never know made him frown. He noticed his mother watching him and attempted to lighten his expression.

Over Emily's shoulder, Aidan nodded hello to Nate then set his daughter down. "Say good night to Grandma and Uncle Nate and I'll tuck you in."

Emily hugged her grandmother then ran up to Nate and put her small arms around his neck. "Good night, Unca Nate. Daddy's going to take me to see you race your bike tomorrow."

"With you cheering for me, I'll be sure to win." He hugged her back. "Sleep well, little Em."

"I'll be right back," Aidan said to Leone and Nate and followed his skipping daughter out of the room.

Leone turned to Nate. "What's wrong? You seem upset. Jim said you came to see him on a job site a few days ago wanting to talk about Angela."

He perched on the edge of one of the hard chairs and leaned forward, his elbows on his knees. "Angela and I had a fight and now she's gone."

"Oh, dear. And I was so hoping…" Leone got up and started tidying away the toys lying around the living room. "What did you fight about—or shouldn't I ask?"

Aidan returned, glanced from troubled face to

troubled face and went to the sideboard to pour shots of neat bourbon for himself and Nate. He picked up a bottle of port and looked questioningly at his mother who shook her head. He handed Nate his drink and sat down opposite him on a love seat. "What's happening?"

"Angela's gone," Leone said quietly.

Aidan sipped his drink and shrugged. "Maybe she had to go to Vancouver for a couple of days for work and didn't get a chance to tell you."

"We had a fight," Nate said tersely. He swirled the amber liquid in the bottom of the heavy crystal glass then took a swig, relishing the burning sensation in his stomach. "She told me she was pregnant when she left ten years ago. She miscarried the same night."

"I'm so sorry," Leone murmured. "I know how much you wanted children. How awful for her to go through that on her own."

"Why didn't she tell you then?" Aidan asked.

Nate leaned forward, his drink cradled between his clenched hands. "She was afraid I'd blame her. She thinks running away caused her to lose the baby. Could it have?" he said, looking at his mother.

Leone shook her head firmly. "*Nothing* will dislodge a healthy baby in the first trimester."

"Not even if the bus she was on was in an accident and she subsequently slipped and fell on an icy street?'' At his mother's gasp of horror, he told them the whole story.

"Not even all that would cause her to lose the baby,'' Leone insisted. "Poor Angela. What a burden she's carried all these years. I'm surprised the nurses in the hospital didn't tell her that.''

"I got the impression she left the hospital as soon as she could, without talking to anyone,'' Nate said.

"You say you fought over this,'' Aidan said. "*Did* you blame her?''

"No.'' Nate got to his feet and paced the room as he struggled to articulate his feelings. "But I wasn't very reassuring. I thought I was falling in love with her again, then this happened and all the old resentments surfaced. I don't know what I feel anymore.''

"Maybe you two aren't meant to be together,'' Aidan said. "Maybe it's time to let her go.''

You let me go. Angela's plaintive words sounded in his heart. Like a child abandoned by her father.

Nate narrowed his eyes at his brother. "You're always telling me you like Angela, that we should be together.''

"I do like her but sticking it out through rough times takes work.'' Aidan shrugged. "Sounds to me as though you don't think she's worth the effort.''

Nate noticed Aidan didn't meet his eyes. Was his brother playing devil's advocate? ''She hasn't exactly given our relationship a vote of confidence. I really think she's run away again. It's the story of our life together.''

''Why does she do that?'' Aidan asked quietly.

''Because she's manipulating me into proving my love.''

''Is that twenty-year-old Nate talking or thirty-year-old Nate?''

Nate looked to his mother for support but Leone merely raised her eyebrows as if Aidan's question was valid. Nate sat down abruptly and turned back to Aidan. ''What's the difference?''

Aidan leveled him a glance over the rim of his glass. ''You tell me.''

''WHAT KIND OF TREE is that?'' Ricky leaned out of Angela's fifth-floor apartment window, arm outstretched as he tried to touch the leaves of a towering elm.

Angela bounded across the living room, grabbed him by the shirt collar and yanked him backward. ''Don't…do…that…again…'' she panted. ''I'll have a heart attack.''

''When are we having dinner? I'm hungry.''

''You're always hungry,'' Angela teased, grabbing him and tickling him until he squealed. Then she remembered that in only fourteen short hours she had to hand him over to his parents. She stopped tickling and hugged him hard. ''Get your shoes on and we'll go out for fish and chips.''

As they left the apartment she double-checked the hall phone to make sure the answering machine was hooked up in case Nate rang while they were gone. Maybe she should have tried harder to let him know she was leaving, but a small voice inside insisted that if he truly wanted her, he would find her.

Be honest, she berated herself. For all her tough talk she didn't have the guts to make the first move. But she'd apologized. What more could she do? She hadn't told him she loved him…but surely he *knew* that. She sighed. Guys probably liked to hear the words, too.

She let Ricky push the elevator button for the ground floor, then grabbed his hand to stop him from punching the button for every floor in between. ''How old are you?'' she scolded, smiling.

''Four,'' he told her with a cheeky grin.

They strolled over to Denman Street then headed north two blocks toward Angela's favorite fish-and-chip shop.

''Look,'' Ricky cried, pointing to an empty storefront where workmen were erecting a sign that read Wilde Ride Mountain Bikes. ''That must be Nate's!''

Angela's heart did a bunny hop. She hadn't realized the store was so close to her apartment. He really would find it convenient to stay with her if… *If.* She hated to think how big an if that might be.

''Why would he want to have a store in the city?'' Ricky wondered.

''This is an ideal location,'' Angela told him. ''He can rent bikes to tourists to ride the seawall around Stanley Park, or to go across the Lion's Gate bridge to the trails on the north shore. Although,'' she added with a shudder, ''from what I've heard about the north shore, you'd have to be either really brave or insanely stupid to ride those trails.''

''Or really good, like Nate,'' Ricky said loyally. ''We'll get back in time to watch his race, won't we?''

''*You* will,'' Angela told him as they moved on. ''We'll pick your mom and dad up at the airport tomorrow and you'll go home with them.''

''What about you?'' Ricky gazed up at her in alarm as if only now realizing she wasn't a permanent fixture in his life.

She stopped at a red light, automatically reaching for his hand to stop him from stepping into the traffic. "I'll stay here. There won't be any room for me at your house with your parents home."

"Oh." Ricky sounded forlorn at the thought. The light changed and they crossed the street. "You could stay with Nate, couldn't you? He's got a big house."

If only life were as simple as it appeared through a ten-year-old's eyes. "I'm not sure he'd want me to live with him."

He'd told her to grow up. Every time she thought of that she burned with resentment and humiliation. Who did he think he was saying that to her? He was *so* wrong.

And yet, her righteous indignation rang false. A niggling voice deep inside told her that maybe, just maybe, he was right.

WEDNESDAY MORNING DAWNED. Nate prepared and ate a prerace breakfast of pancakes and fruit but his heart wasn't in the competition that was to take place at two o'clock that day. He was starting to feel very bad about some of the things he'd said to Angela. Was his attitude just as much to blame as he thought hers was? Had he learned nothing about relationships in ten years? Was he going to let pride stand in the way of his happiness?

When he thought back to himself at twenty he had to concede he'd been somewhat selfish, a little arrogant and altogether more concerned with his pride than with listening to Angela's needs.

Why *should* she have believed in him? He'd shown no initiative in those days for anything but biking; how could she have known his consuming passion would eventually pay off? Not even he'd been sure at the time where it would lead. As for having a child... There his thoughts faltered. Their lost child still hurt and probably always would. But if he loved her, he should be able to forgive her.

And he *did* love her.

Underneath that tough-chick exterior beat the heart of a scared, vulnerable girl. A girl who was still waiting for her daddy to come home. He wasn't her father and he had no intention of filling that role—nor did he think she wanted him to—but he was damned if he was going to be another man in her life who'd let her down.

Face it, when it came to Angela, pride was a luxury he couldn't afford. If she needed reassurance he should give it to her. If he really loved her he should be willing to prove it over and over until she couldn't help but believe.

Nate picked up the phone and dialed the number at Janice's house. He listened to the phone ring out in disbelief. A glance at his watch told him it was only seven-thirty. Where could she be at this time? He hoped Ricky hadn't had another emergency, or that if he had, Angela would know she could call him.

He put on his biking shorts and T-shirt and rode down Alta Lake Road, looping back on the Valley Trail to warm up and to take his mind off Angela. When he got back forty-five minutes later he tried calling her again but there was still no answer. If her house hadn't been dark and her car gone last night he might not have thought too much of it. Given the circumstances he began to worry that she really had taken off.

He called Kerry but she hadn't seen Angela since the day before when she'd picked up Ricky after his sleepover with Tim. Still troubled but not knowing what else to do, Nate loaded his Balfa into the back of his Jeep and drove to the bike shop. Angela was an adult. If she wanted to go somewhere with her nephew she had every right to do so.

Parking at the back, he wheeled the Balfa into the workshop. "Yo, Kevin," he called to his mechanic. "Mind checking over my bike before the race?"

Kevin straightened away from the frame he was working on and came over, scratching his chest through his white T-shirt. "I thought you took care of your own machines."

"I tuned and lubed it last night but..." Nate

shook his head. "I've been a little distracted lately and I'd like you to go over it, as well, in case I missed a loose bolt or something."

"Sure thing, boss."

Nate went to his cubbyhole office to wait, and to see if any message had come in from Angela. A tap at the doorframe heralded the arrival of Rachel. He scooted backward on his wheeled chair and she dropped a stack of letters on his desk, eyeing him curiously. "You look like hell. Didn't you sleep last night?"

"Not much." It was bound to affect his performance today but except for the sake of the Children's Hospital he couldn't work up the energy to care. If he lost, he'd figure out some other way to help the kids.

"Someone's got a girlfriend," Rachel teased in a singsong voice.

Nate picked up the mail, hoping she'd take the hint and leave. When she didn't, he glared up at her. "Don't you have work to do?"

"I'm doing it." She tossed a color brochure from a prominent mountain-bike company on his desk. "A new line of shocks have just come out that look really ace. I think we should order them."

He flipped through the supply catalog while Rachel gave him the rundown on the shocks, impressing Nate as usual with her efficiency and attention to detail.

"They sound fine. Go ahead and order whatever you think we can move by the end of the summer," he said when she'd finished. She turned to go but he called her back. "I need a manager for my Vancouver store, someone competent I can trust. Would you be interested?"

"Me?" she squeaked, clasping her clipboard to her chest as a grin spread across her face. "Manager?"

Nate smiled for the first time in days. "You practically run this place anyway."

"Oh, goody! Thank you so much." She bounced on her toes. Then realizing she wasn't acting professionally, came back to earth, sober faced. "I mean, I appreciate the opportunity you're offering me."

Laughing, Nate leaned back in his chair. "Never curb your enthusiasm, Rachel. At least not around me."

Rachel left, still grinning broadly. Nate dialed Angela's number, glancing at his watch as he did so. Nearly one o'clock. He'd have to get up to the mountain soon.

After so many fruitless attempts to contact her he was surprised when she said hello on the third ring. He sat forward abruptly, his chair legs coming down on the floor with a thump. "Angela. Where've you been?"

"This is *Janice,* not Angela." Janice laughed, and even their laughs sounded similar. "That's the second time in the past twenty minutes someone's made that mistake."

Nate struggled to collect himself. "Janice. This is Nate. I didn't know you were back."

"We came home early. Didn't Angela tell you?"

"No, where is she? I've been calling all morning."

"As far as I know she's in Vancouver. Unless the guy from the *Globe and Mail* got hold of her and she decided to jump on a plane to Toronto. He called here earlier and thinking I was Angela, offered me a job. I almost accepted, except I knew I'd never get away with it."

"The job in Toronto? She decided not to take it."

"Oh?" Janice sounded suddenly cautious, if not downright cagey, setting alarm bells off in Nate's head. "She might have changed her mind, what with recent events…"

Nate groaned. "Do you really think she's flying out there?"

"I wouldn't know," Janice said, although her tone suggested she had her suspicions. "Excuse me a sec—'' Nate could hear voices in the background on her end of the line and she came back to say, ''Sorry, Nate, I'd better go. Ricky's anxious to get up the mountain to watch your race.''

''Oh hell.'' Nate raked a hand through his hair. ''Tell Ricky I'm sorry but I've just decided to scratch. What's Angela's address in Vancouver? And don't try and fob me off by saying she told you not to give it to me. This is important.''

''I wouldn't dream of fobbing you off. Have you got a pen and paper?''

He hung up after writing down the information and tried Angela's apartment phone number. No answer. Nor was she at her workplace. Either she was on her way to Toronto or she'd gone out for a newspaper or something and would be back soon. Whichever, he wasn't going to sit around Whistler waiting to find out.

He loaded his bike back in his Jeep, left instructions with Rachel to notify race organizers he wouldn't be at the starting gate and took off out of Whistler, heading south to Vancouver.

CHAPTER FIFTEEN

ANGELA WALKED DOWN to Lost Lagoon at the entrance to Stanley Park and sat on a park bench, staring at the fountain in the middle of the lake.

Janice and Bob had gone straight home, taking Ricky with them, and she felt more alone than ever. She hadn't wanted to go east again but the job offer was a perfect way out of a sticky emotional situation seeing as how things weren't going to work out with Nate—

Hold it right there, she told herself firmly. Who said things weren't going to work out? Why give up so easily?

Because that's what she did. At least where Nate was concerned. She was always asking him, directly or indirectly, to prove his devotion to her but when had she ever put herself on the line for him?

But he'd let her go.

Grow up, she told herself. *Get over it.*

It was time she learned to take their love on trust

and not expect him to shoulder the emotional burden of her past.

He loved her. She loved him.

Sometimes life really was that simple.

TRAFFIC ON THE SOUTHBOUND LANE of Highway 99 was light and Nate was making good time, inching above the speed limit on the straight stretches. For the most part though the road twisted and turned, rose and fell, hugging the rock face rising steeply on his left.

Nate pulled out his cell phone and tried Angela's Vancouver number again. No answer. If she still wasn't there when he got to her apartment he would camp out in his Jeep until she came home. And if it turned out she'd gone to Toronto he would get on a plane and follow her. This time she wasn't getting away.

Still with the phone to his ear, he hauled on the steering wheel one-handed as he went around a tight corner. Then swore under his breath at the sight of rocks tumbling down the steep slope right across the narrow two-lane highway. Tossing the phone, he gripped the wheel with both hands and applied his brakes, knowing he had no hope of stopping or of avoiding all the rocks. To make matters worse a car heading north in the opposite lane had veered to the far right. It managed to squeak past on the gravel shoulder but Nate was forced to pass it on the wrong side, straight into the path of the rock slide. A chunk of mountain the size of a basketball hit the side of the truck with a loud thump. Swerving and cursing, he tried to avoid rolling boulders ahead. Smaller rocks crashed down on the windshield, cracking the glass right in his line of vision.

Hitting something was inevitable. The grinding crunch of metal on granite brought his Jeep to a jolting halt. When the dust settled the vehicle was tilted to one side and slewed at an angle just inches from the rock face.

Nate climbed out and crouched to peer underneath to inspect the damage. What he saw made him curse so loudly a bluejay sitting in a pine by the roadside flew off, squawking. Nate kicked the tire in impotent rage. The sump was punctured and leaking oil. He would have to get towed out of here.

Meanwhile, Angela could be making decisions that took her far away from him. Even if she wasn't planning on taking the *Globe and Mail* job, she would be thinking he didn't care about her enough to forgive and forget.

He had to get to her and there was only one way—on his bike.

He wrote a note and left it on the dash for the

police. Luckily the Jeep was far enough off the road and past the main area of the rock slide that he wouldn't obstruct traffic or a cleanup crew.

Minutes later he had the Balfa unloaded, his helmet strapped on and he was flying down the highway. Illogical or not, now that he was on his bike he felt as though everything was going to be okay. This wasn't a race but it could turn out to be the most important ride of his life.

Thinking about racing made him glance at his watch. Right about now he should have been launching himself out of the starting gate. He felt a slight pang knowing he would never add that trophy to his collection, but he didn't regret scratching, not when he thought of what he stood to gain.

He figured the ride to Vancouver would take a couple hours since the road was dry and the route mostly downhill. He was warmed up now and feeling good, his legs pumping strongly, his lungs clear and breathing deeply. He wasn't making as good time as he would have in the truck but he would get there.

He'd just passed the town of Squamish when a blue Subaru flashed by on the other side, did a U-turn and came after him, honking its horn.

For crying out loud, some yahoos just couldn't leave cyclists alone. Riding as close to the shoulder as he could, he motioned the Subaru to pass. It pulled over and stopped directly in his path. Nate checked behind him for following traffic in preparation for swinging wide of the parked car, then glanced back. The driver's door opened.

Out stepped Angela.

She had on the pink-and-green flowered dress she'd worn to his mother's birthday and the breeze lifted her blond hair away from her tanned bare shoulders.

For the second time that day, Nate applied his brakes in a hurry, skidding to a stop in the gravel at the side of the road a yard away from her.

"You're a little off course." She gave him her cheekiest smile.

Heart pounding from emotion as much as exertion, Nate unlatched his helmet and struggled to act casual. *Keep a lid on, Wilde. Don't blow it now.* "Is that all you have to say after almost running me down?"

Her smile trembled and her eyes grew wide and vulnerable. "No, I have something much more important to say. Nate, I—I love you."

To hell with playing it cool. Letting his precious Balfa crash to the ground, he took a giant step and gathered her in his embrace. "No one's ever going to hurt you again, least of all me."

"I'm sorry." Her arms tightened around his neck. "So sorry I didn't tell you about our baby."

"Shh, it wasn't your fault. I was to blame. I didn't give you what you needed." He drew back to look at her. "Don't ever run away again because if you do, I'm going to be coming after you."

Her smile glimmered beneath her tears. "Even to Toronto?"

"You're not going to Toronto. I don't care if they hand you the newspaper on a platter. You belong in Whistler with me."

"I know. I'm moving back. I have an idea for job sharing with Penny that I plan to run by Denise. Whether you want me to live with you, or not, I'm going to be near you. Everyone who matters to me—you, my sister and your family—is there. But mostly you." She sighed. "I'm sorry about the whole divorce thing."

"I'm not. There's nothing like the death knell to focus your thoughts. If not for the prospect of losing you forever I might not have woken up to how much I love you."

Her eyes lit. "You really love me?"

"You know I do. And I'll never again be too proud to admit I need you. And baby, *I need you.*" He kissed her again, long and lingering, barely noticing as passing cars tooted their horns at them.

"I'm sorry you're not going to get your trophy," she said when they paused to breathe.

"I won something far more important—you." He raised her hand to kiss her fingers and felt a ring on her third finger. "You still have your wedding band?" he said, incredulous.

"If you gave me any trouble I was going to remind you of your promise to me, the one you had inscribed inside the ring."

"'Yours until the mountains crumble to the sea,'" he quoted softly. With the snow-tipped mountains on one side and the blue waters of Howe Sound on the other, the wording was particularly apt. "But do you realize that just up the road the mountain actually is crumbling into the ocean?" he said in a lighter tone, and told her about the rock slide and the punctured sump in his Jeep.

"You're not getting out of it that easily," she warned, grinning.

"Oh, I don't know. I'll bet a good lawyer could make the case stand up in court," he teased, rubbing noses.

"We're back, aren't we?" Her eyes were shining.

"We're back, and we're staying together."

A shadow passed across her face. "You don't think we'll have problems again?"

"What married couple doesn't argue sometimes? But we're communicating now at a level we never did when we were younger." He smoothed back her hair, wanting to touch her, hold her, possess her.

"We do have a lot in common," Angela added, coming up with her own reasons for them to have a successful marriage. "We like each other as well as being in love."

"Absolutely. But don't forget good old-fashioned lust." His body hardened just thinking about making love with Angela.

"Nate," she murmured when his hand strayed to her breasts. "We're in full view of passing traffic."

Nate shifted his grip to a more respectable location on her waist. "We're going to be one of those couples who when they're eighty years old, sit on the couch holding hands in front of their grandchildren's video camera and reminisce about—"

"—their courtship," she said with a dreamy smile.

Nate nodded. "Finishing each other's sentences and—"

"—laughing at each other's jokes—"

"—even when they've heard them a million times."

Her eyes narrowed in a cute little frown. "Hmm. Don't know about *that*."

"We'll have a dozen grandchildren," he said turning to other important matters.

"Don't we need children first?" Angela suggested.

"Good idea. It's about time we started that family. After we get a tow truck we'll go back to my house—"

"Our house, don't you mean?"

That simple phrase brought home to Nate the full import of the love and happiness that was coming his way. "Our house," he repeated.

As they packed his bike in the trunk of her car, his mind flitted briefly to the last entry in his mental list. *Advantage of Bachelorhood Number 152* was a big blank.

Time to start a new list.

Advantage of Marriage Number 1: Angela.

*   *   *   *   *

Watch for Family Matters,
the next installment in
THE WILDE MEN
trilogy featuring Marc.
Coming in September 2004.

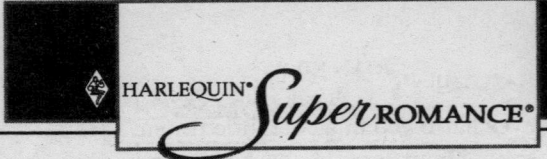
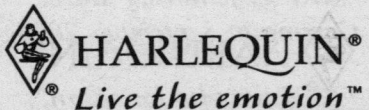

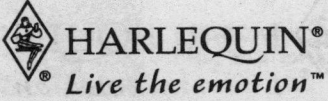

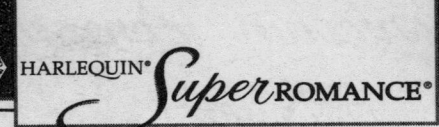

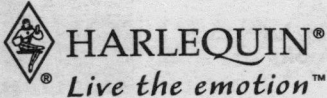

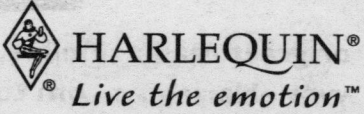